Is Chelsea Going Blind?

Alida E. Young

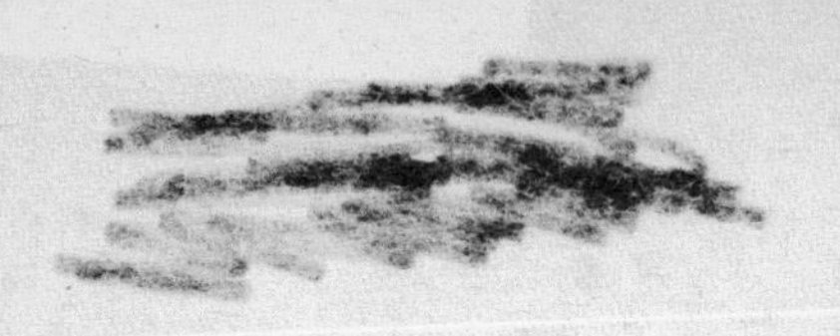

Cover photo by John Strange

Published by Willowisp Press, Inc.
401 E. Wilson Bridge Road, Worthington, Ohio 43085

Originally published as *I'll Be Seeing You*

Printed in the United States of America

10 9 8 7 6 5 4 3 2 1

ISBN 0-87406-367-1

To the memory of my mother, Ellen Quick, and to my dear friend, Loeta Marcum, two of the most courageous women I have ever known.

For their help, special thanks to Jimmy, Cathy, Roman, and Sylvia.

My thanks and appreciation to Richard J. Salem Esq.; Fortune Zuckerman, Director of Braille Institute in Palm Springs; James M. Rachford, O.D.; John Stocking; Rosa Lee Fabricius; Molly Morton; Gary Dunaway; Marti Nelson; Char Whitaker; Jill Koom; Robert McGrath; Joe Wright, Swim Coach at Palm Springs High School, and his son Tim; and to all the teachers, counselors, and librarians of the Morongo Basin.

And for their special encouragement, thanks to the 5th and 6th graders and their teachers at Joshua Tree Elementary School.

One

"I'M starved," Chelsea said. "Let's eat lunch."

Chelsea Moore and her best friend Tina Webb spread out a blanket on the ground. Chelsea switched on the radio to her favorite station. "I love this place," she said. "It's like we're in an enchanted forest."

They both looked around. Ferns grew everywhere. Pollen darted in the few shafts of light that filtered through the dense stand of trees. They were only about five miles from Seaview, but the glade was like another world.

"Yeah," Tina said. "It's like those fairy tales we used to read. I keep expecting a prince to appear."

Chelsea laughed. "With our luck, he'd turn out to be the Frog Prince."

"I know a couple of guys I wish would turn into frogs," Tina said.

"Kevin and Mickey?" Chelsea asked, but she

already knew the answer.

"Right. They think they're so smart because they'll be going into the tenth grade this fall. And we'll still be in junior high—just poor dumb freshmen."

Kevin Gerrard and Mickey Calhoun both lived near Chelsea. She'd had a crush on Kevin since the third grade. Tina tried to pretend she didn't like Mickey, but Chelsea knew better. Chelsea dug out a cheese sandwich from her lunch sack. "I hate for summer to end," she said. "It's been the very best summer I can ever remember." She and Tina had Saturdays off now, but when school started they would work for Tina's dad on Saturdays. Chelsea sighed. "No more days at the beach, no more all-day horseback rides, no more—"

"No more picking ferns," Tina finished for her. "Studying has to be easier than working."

Every summer Chelsea earned money by helping Tina's family gather ferns and evergreens. The Webbs owned a florist shop with a nursery and greenhouses. Mr. Webb and Tina's two older brothers were picking evergreens a little deeper in the woods.

"Oh, I don't know," Chelsea said. "I like being able to buy my photographic materials." Someday she hoped to be a photographer, but it was an expensive hobby.

Tina finished her peanut butter and jelly sandwich and stood up to stretch.

"Hold it, Tina. Don't move. I want to get a shot of you."

"Don't you get tired of taking pictures?" Tina asked, but Chelsea could tell that her friend was pleased. Chelsea quickly wiped her hands on her jeans and got out her camera.

"Is my hair okay?" Tina wanted to know. "Wait, let me tuck in my shirt."

"You look perfect." Chelsea looked through the viewfinder and tried to focus on Tina, but something was the matter. She closed her eyes, blinked a few times, and tried again. Things still looked slightly blurry.

"My arms are getting tired. What's wrong?"

Chelsea looked up and everything seemed to be all right again. "Nothing," she said, snapping one quick shot. "I guess I got grease from my cheese sandwich on the lens."

Tina groaned and put down her arms. "Well, if you're through eating, we'd better get back to work." Tina picked up her empty lunch sack and wadded it up. She aimed it at Chelsea, catching her on the side of the head. "Gotcha!"

"Hey, cut that out!" Chelsea set her camera down and threw her sack at Tina. For a few minutes the sacks were sailing furiously back and forth until Tina's was in shreds.

"Ha! I won," Chelsea said.

Tina grinned. "Next time I'll bring my dad's lunch pail."

Chelsea was laughing, but she was still a bit worried about her camera. She didn't want to have to spend money on a new lens. She hurriedly put away the camera and began helping Tina lay out some gunny sacks.

Chelsea slipped a ring knife on her finger and began to clip the tough woody stem of a sword fern. She stripped a few of the fronds off the bottom, then held the fern in her left hand while she cut another.

Without looking up, Tina asked, "Do you think Kevin will have another end-of-summer party this year?"

"Probably. But will he ask us?"

"I hope so. I saw the greatest outfit at Teen Alley. Maybe it'll be on sale next month."

Tina loved to buy new clothes, especially the latest fads. She was small and dark-haired. And she had a cute figure that looked good in almost anything. Chelsea wasn't unhappy with her own looks. Her long brown hair had enough curl in it to be easy to manage. And lots of people commented on her gray eyes and heart-shaped face. But she didn't care all that much about clothes. She liked to be comfortable.

Chelsea and Tina worked in silence for a

while. When Chelsea had picked twenty-five ferns, she tied the bunch with fern string. Then she stacked the bunches on the gunny sack strip and pinned them on with a nail.

When the strip was filled with ferns, Tina rolled it up like a jelly roll and tied it onto a packboard.

By four o'clock when Mr. Webb came to load the ferns on the truck, Chelsea was exhausted. She and Tina climbed up front in the cab. On the ride home Tina chattered away, but Chelsea closed her eyes and half dozed until they came into town.

She roused up and thought her eyes had gone crazy, until she realized it was fog. Wisps of gray swirled in from the ocean, settling into the low gullies.

Mr. Webb dropped Chelsea off at her drive. "Thanks, Chelsea," he said. "You're a good worker. You girls picked 160 bunches today."

"We'll do 170 tomorrow," Chelsea said.

Tina groaned. "Speak for yourself."

Chelsea slung her camera over her shoulder. Wearily, she climbed down from the truck.

"Call me later," Tina said. "Okay?"

Chelsea nodded. If I can still move by then, she thought. For the last few weeks she'd felt more tired than usual, especially when she'd had to use her eyes a lot. She waved at the departing truck and headed for the house.

Through the thickening mists came a bounding dark figure. "Hey, Midnight." The black lab wagged his tail wildly and squeaked happy little yips of joy. As if he had radar or something, the dog was always there to meet her.

Chelsea followed Midnight down the path to the house, which was almost hidden by the swirling gray fog.

* * * * *

After a long bath Chelsea felt better, but when she was brushing her hair, her reflection in the mirror blurred. She wiped the mirror. It wasn't the steam, it was definitely her eyes. For the last couple of weeks, her eyes had hurt and burned when she used them too much. She was never ill, but lately she'd had headaches and almost felt sick to her stomach whenever she tried to read. She hated the idea of glasses even though she knew plenty of kids who wore them—grown-ups, too. Even her father wore glasses.

Chelsea went out to the kitchen where her mother was scrubbing potatoes. "Hi, Mom," she said brightly, so her mother wouldn't guess anything was wrong. "What's for dinner?"

"Meat loaf and baked potatoes. That fog is

cold and damp, so an oven meal sounds good tonight. You're just in time to fix the zucchini."

Chelsea liked having her mother home for the summer. Her mom was a counselor at Seaview High. Sometimes Chelsea wasn't too thrilled with the idea that the junior and senior highs were on the same campus. Still, if she really needed her mother, she'd be handy.

Chelsea washed the zucchini. "Where's Sharon? I thought this was her day to help."

"She's at Eric's. They're rehearsing."

Eric Hastings was Sharon's latest boyfriend. He had a rock band, and sometimes Sharon sang with them. She'd be going away to college this fall. Chelsea smiled to herself. Soon she'd have the whole bedroom to herself.

"Where's Billy?" Chelsea asked. "He's supposed to set the table."

"He's at baseball practice. He'll be home in a few minutes."

When Chelsea finished helping with dinner, she looked out the kitchen window at the sea of fog. She couldn't see the surf below nor the rocks at the beach. For a moment she had the strangest feeling that the gray swirls would come into the room and smother her. She had to laugh at herself. A little eyestrain was making her weird.

* * * * *

"We haven't had a summer pea-souper like this in years," Chelsea's father said as he helped himself to a second serving of zucchini. "It came in so fast. I thought I'd never get home."

Chelsea's dad was a tax consultant and business manager. He had a mind with five tracks that could work all at once. Chelsea wished she were more like him. But actually, she wasn't like any of the rest of the family. Her nine-year-old brother, Billy, looked exactly like their dad—except for the mustache, of course. They both had curly brown hair and blue-gray eyes. And Sharon looked so much like their mother that people asked if they were sisters. They were both five foot four with golden brown hair and eyes to match. Chelsea didn't look like anyone else in her family. When she was little she had thought somebody must have switched the babies at the hospital when she was born.

Chelsea stared down at the food on her plate. It all seemed to run together. She only half listened to her family's chatter about the events of the day. Sometimes she envied Tina. The Webbs ate on TV trays in front of the television. But Chelsea's father insisted that the Moore family eat at least one meal together in the dining room.

Chelsea's dad was telling a funny story about a client. Chelsea was pretty sure he had made it up. Her mother had spent the day at a shelter for battered kids. All Sharon could talk about was Eric and his band. And Billy went on and on about his dumb baseball team. The voices sounded muffled and far away.

"Chelsea? How was your day?" her father asked. "How many bundles of ferns did you pick?"

"What?" Chelsea looked up, startled.

"Are you all right?" her mother asked. "You haven't touched your food."

"I'm just not hungry, Mom," she said quickly.

"I think you're working too hard," her father said. "And I don't like you being out in those woods."

They had been through this argument a dozen times. "Sure, Dad, Big Foot might get me."

"Don't get smart, young lady."

"I'm sorry, but I need the money. There are hardly any jobs for kids."

"I suppose you're right," he said. "But I'd feel better if you did baby-sitting or something like that."

* * * * *

After dinner, Chelsea's dad went into his study. He always had a lot of work to do at night. Her mom was in the living room reading, and Sharon was on the phone, as usual. That was one more reason Chelsea would be glad when Sharon went off to college.

"Want to play some ping-pong?" Billy asked Chelsea.

"I'm too tired. I worked all day, you know."

"Then how about a game of backgammon?"

Chelsea loved games. If she said no, her mother would wonder why. "Sure. But don't cry when I beat you." They set up the board on the dining room table. Billy loved games, too. But he was so full of energy, he could never sit still for very long. They'd only been playing for a while when he got up and stretched his arms high in the air. He looked like he was trying to stretch his five foot three inch body to six foot nine. His dream was to be a pro basketball player.

"Sis, can I borrow your camera tomorrow?" he asked.

"I'm sorry, but I think there's something wrong with the focus or the lens."

"But I said I'd take pictures of the team. Please, Chelsea."

"No, you might mess it up. I saved a whole year to buy that camera."

"Okay, then you can't play my backgammon

game if I can't use your camera."

"I don't want to play anymore." Somehow the spots on the dice weren't clear. It took an effort to focus her eyes. "Anyway," she said, "Sharon's finally off the phone."

"Aw, come on, just one more game," Billy pleaded.

"I have to call Tina."

"Cripes, you were with her all day. Women! God should have made all of you with a telephone stuck to your head."

Chelsea ignored him and went to the kitchen phone where she'd have more privacy. She dialed, and Tina answered.

"I was beginning to think you weren't going to call," Tina said. "Pop told me to tell you we won't be picking brush tomorrow."

Chelsea was sorry to lose the money, but not sorry to get a day off. "What'll we do tomorrow?"

"Let's go swimming."

"Not if it's foggy like this." Chelsea tried to think of something where she wouldn't have to use her eyes. "Come on over, and let's listen to tapes. Sharon just bought me a new one."

"Boy, if you get many more, you're going to have to build a new house."

Chelsea had a huge collection of tapes and records, mostly rock music. She even had some of the very first rock and roll records that her dad had given her from his collection.

Chelsea and Tina talked for a while about their friends—especially the boys. After a few minutes, Chelsea pretended to yawn. "I'm so sleepy, Tina. I'll see you tomorrow? Okay?"

"Yeah, I'm beat, too. We really worked hard. See you in the morning."

As Chelsea replaced the receiver, the dog came up to her and rubbed against her leg, wanting to be petted. She held his face in her hands. He stared at her with his big brownish-yellow eyes.

"Okay, Midnight, tell me the honest truth. How do you think I'd look in glasses?"

Two

FOR the next week or so, Chelsea tried to pretend that nothing was wrong. She made excuses to be alone. She told Mr. Webb that she'd looked at the sun too long, that her eyes needed rest. She wouldn't play ping-pong or other games with Billy. She even avoided Tina. With Midnight as her only companion, she spent the days listening to her music, horseback riding, and walking along the beach. Sometimes she left the private beach and stopped to watch kids surfing or playing volleyball. But mostly she stayed to herself.

One morning a couple of Saturdays later, the doorbell rang.

Chelsea answered the door to find Tina standing on the porch with her hands on her hips. "Are you trying to avoid me?" Tina asked. "You haven't returned my phone calls. Did I do something to make you mad?"

"No, of course not," Chelsea answered. "I've

just had a lot of headaches."

"The tide's in, but I guess you don't feel like going swimming. . . ."

Tina looked so forlorn that Chelsea said, "Sure I do. Come on in. I'll pack us a lunch, and we can stay on the beach all day. Did you bring your suit?"

Tina grinned, reached down behind a bush, and pulled out her canvas tote bag. " 'Always be prepared' is my motto."

They fixed sandwiches and chose some tapes to take with them. With Midnight at their heels, they headed for the beach.

The air smelled briney and fresh. Gulls screeched overhead, and a one-legged sandpiper hopped across the firm, wet sand. Midnight playfully ran in circles . . . chasing a bird, chasing a wave, chasing his tail.

Chelsea and Tina secured their things by a driftwood log. Then they raced each other out into the water. Chelsea gasped as a wave broke over her. Even in summer the water was icy. They swam out past the breakers. Tina was a good swimmer. But she wasn't as strong as Chelsea, who was faster and could swim farther without tiring.

The two of them spent most of the morning body surfing, riding the waves into shore.

"Next year, Dad says I can get a surfboard," Tina said, as they rested for a few minutes before swimming back out.

"I've asked, but you know my dad. I'll probably be a hundred and fifty before he lets me have a board."

"Are you going to try out for the swim team this year?" Tina asked.

"You bet—if it's okay with my mom and dad. It costs quite a bit by the time you buy a suit and warm-ups and a parka and a cap and goggles. . . ."

"Some day, I'm going to be a millionaire," Tina said, dreamily.

"And you'd probably spend it all on clothes."

Tina made a face and threw a handful of wet sand at Chelsea. "Come on, let's swim some more before the tide turns."

By lunchtime they were tired and hungry.

Because the day was unusually warm, they sat on the sand in the shade of a rock to eat their sandwiches—sandywiches, Tina called them.

Midnight came running up from the sea. He stopped right in front of Tina and shook himself.

"Oh! You rotten dog. Chelsea, did you teach him that? He never gets you all wet."

Chelsea just grinned and tossed Midnight a dog treat.

After they ate, they walked barefooted in

the damp sand at the edge of the water. They liked to hunt for water-filled seaweed bulbs. Whenever Tina stepped on one it popped like a firecracker. Every one that Chelsea stepped on went *ploosh.*

"Hey, look," Tina said and pointed to the cliff.

Chelsea turned and squinted, but she couldn't see anything. "Look at what?"

"Two people on four-wheeled cycles are coming down the hill. They're crazy! That hill's steep."

Because she couldn't see them, Chelsea pretended uninterest.

"Oh, it's Kevin and Mickey," Tina said. "Maybe they'll come over here."

"I could care less," Chelsea said, trying to sound casual. "Come on, let's go back in the water."

"Phooey, they're headed the other way."

There was only a two-mile stretch of private beach where kids could ride bikes or dune buggies or all-terrain cycles. But it was so difficult to reach that the beach was usually deserted. Now, Kevin and his friends would be tearing up and down on their bikes, spoiling everything.

The tide was going out now, so Chelsea and Tina didn't go swimming again. Chelsea was tempted to take Tina through the cave to her special rock, but she wanted one place in the whole world that was hers alone.

"What time do you have?" Tina asked. "I'm supposed to be home at two-thirty."

Chelsea didn't want Tina to realize how difficult it was to read the time. "My watch has stopped," she said.

"I guess I'd better go," Tina said sadly. "Coming?"

"I think I'll take a few pictures. Call me later."

Chelsea waved. As soon as Tina was out of sight, she whistled for Midnight to follow her to her favorite spot. It was a large, barnacle-covered rock.

From the top of the bluff or from the beach it was hidden from view. Chelsea had to reach it by going through a cave to a rocky cove. She loved to sit there when the tide went out to take pictures of the sea creatures left in the tide pools. Sometimes she was even lucky enough to get a shot of a sea lion catching fish.

She switched on her radio and watched the dog chase sandpipers and seagulls for a while. The sun was getting low in the west. Chelsea glanced at her watch, but she still could hardly make out the numbers. Her eyes were definitely getting worse. Frightened now, she picked up her things and scrambled off the rock. As she came out of the narrow cave, she saw Kevin on his four-wheeled cycle. The beach looked deserted. Kevin was racing up a sand dune and didn't see her until he turned around. He came zooming up to her, made a fast turn, and tipped over.

Laughing now, Chelsea quickly got out her camera to take a picture of him sprawled on the sand. "Don't move," she said.

Kevin sat up and stared at her as if she were a ghost. "Where in the world did you come from? I didn't see a soul on the beach."

Chelsea made a vague gesture toward a sand dune. "You were too busy with that bike."

Midnight was trying to lick Kevin's face. Kevin laughed. "Don't try to soft soap me, you mutt."

She took one picture and moved the film-wind lever for a second shot. The lever stopped midway. Out of film! She frowned. The last time she'd used it, she'd had several frames left. Billy! That little twerp had used her camera, after all. Angry now, she started off toward home with Midnight at her heels.

"Hey, what's the matter?" Kevin asked. "What'd I do?"

"Nothing," she yelled over the sound of the surf.

Chelsea hurried up the long flight of steps. Twice she nearly fell. She charged into the house. "Where's Billy?" she asked her mother. "I'm going to wring his little neck."

"He's helping me carry in the the food. And where have you been? Everyone's at the table."

"I was down at the beach."

"Well, get washed up. And hurry."

Chelsea put her things away. By the time she was ready, her family had started without her. She took her seat next to Billy and whispered, "How come you took my camera after I told you not to?"

"I didn't hurt it. I just took a couple of pictures of the team. I was going to put in a brand new roll of film today."

"Will you two stop whispering," their father said. "If it's so important, let us hear, too."

Chelsea glared at Billy, who knew their father would refuse to listen to tattling unless it was serious. And she knew her father wouldn't consider this serious. "It's nothing, Dad."

Billy gave her a smug look. Just as she took an ear of corn and buttered it, Billy said, "Hey, Sis, pass the butter."

Chelsea put down the corn, licked her greasy fingers and wiped them on her napkin.

"Boy, are you slow," Billy complained. "Come on, my corn's getting cold."

"If you don't like it, get it yourself."

"Yeah, and get bawled out for reaching. Mom!"

"Chelsea! Billy! Stop that bickering. For the last couple of weeks, all you two do is argue."

"She starts it," Billy whined.

"I do not! You're just a—"

"That's enough out of both of you," their father said quietly. "Chelsea, pass your brother the butter."

Angrily, Chelsea reached for the butter dish. Her vision blurred and she stuck her hand into the soft butter.

"Oh, yuck!" Sharon said.

"And you call me a slob. Man, are you blind or something?" Billy asked sarcastically.

At the word blind, Chelsea's heart seemed to stop for a second. What would I do if I couldn't see? she thought. What if I were blind!

As she handed Billy the dish, she knocked over his glass of milk. It sloshed into his lap.

He yelled and jumped up. "Dad! She did that on purpose."

"I didn't. My hand was slippery."

"You did it on purpose just 'cause I used your dumb old camera."

"All right!" she yelled. "I did it on purpose. Now, are you satisfied?" She burst into tears and ran out of the room.

Midnight came running up. But as if he

knew she were upset, he quietly followed her to her room. She lay huddled on her bed, crying softly.

After a few minutes her mother knocked on the door. "Chelsea, I want to talk to you."

Chelsea gulped back a sob. "I can't talk now, Mom. Tomorrow."

"No, right now."

Her mother came into the room and sat on the foot of Chelsea's twin bed. "Now, I want to know what's wrong."

Chelsea wiped her eyes on the edge of her bedspread. "Nothing's wrong."

"Honey, don't tell me that. You don't burst into tears just because you spill some milk." Her mother put her hand on Chelsea's forehead. "You must be coming down with something."

"Oh, Mom, it's my eyes. I don't want to wear glasses."

Her mother let out a deep sigh. "Oh, Chelsea, why didn't you tell us you were having trouble seeing? I know it must seem terrible to you, but maybe you'll only have to wear glasses to read. Or maybe you can wear contact lenses."

Her mother gathered Chelsea in her arms. "First thing Monday, we'll get an appointment with Dr. Peterson. Glasses won't be so bad. You'll see."

* * * * *

Her father's optometrist was able to see Chelsea on Monday afternoon. But after several tests he made an appointment for Chelsea to see an ophthalmologist.

"Dr. Myers can fit you in as soon as he finishes with a patient. He's right here in this building."

"But what's wrong?" Chelsea wanted to know. "Aren't you going to give me glasses?"

"I'm not sure glasses will help your condition, Chelsea. Dr. Myers will be able to tell you."

Chelsea and her mother were silent as they rode up the elevator to the eighth floor. The waiting room was empty except for an old man with glasses so thick they looked as if they were made out of a cola bottle. Chelsea picked up a magazine, but the pages were just a blur. She tried to keep her voice steady as she asked, "Mom, how come Dr. Peterson didn't just give me glasses. How come I have to go to a medical doctor? Mom—I'm scared."

Before her mother could answer, Chelsea's father burst in. "Rod Peterson's receptionist called me. She said you two were waiting to see an eye doctor. Madelyn, what's wrong? What did Peterson say?"

Chelsea's mother shrugged. "Nothing much.

He doesn't think glasses will help."

He sank down on the couch beside Chelsea. "Are you okay, sweetheart?"

Chelsea blinked back the tears that threatened to spill over. But she managed to say, "Sure, Daddy, I'm fine."

* * * * *

After more tests, Dr. Myers called Chelsea's parents into his office. Chelsea sat frozen, not understanding everything the doctor said. She had something called optic nerve atrophy.

"How serious is it?" her father asked.

"It may or may not get worse. It can go to total blindness. There's just no way of predicting."

No one said anything for a long moment. Then her father slammed his hand on the desk, startling Chelsea.

"It can't be true! There must be a mistake."

"There's no mistake, Mr. Moore. I'm sorry to be so blunt, but it's better that you face up to it. Often the side vision goes first, but in Chelsea's case, it's the center vision."

"What about an operation?" Chelsea's mother asked in a stunned voice.

"I'll make an appointment for her at the Eye Institute in Bay City. They'll investigate the cause. It can be hereditary, or it can be caused by a tumor. If it's caused by a tumor, an operation might help."

"Well, I want the very best doctors available," her father said.

Her mother gathered Chelsea in her arms. "Honey, it's going to be all right."

* * * * *

The next week when they were leaving for the three-hour drive to the Eye Institute, Sharon and Billy looked more upset than Chelsea felt.

Sharon gave her a hug. "Don't worry, little sister."

Billy gave Chelsea a light punch on the arm. "I'm sorry I borrowed your camera. I got you a whole extra roll of film and everything."

Chelsea blinked back the tears that always seemed ready to flow lately. "Thanks. See you guys in a couple of days."

On the drive to Bay City, everybody was trying to sound cheerful, but Chelsea knew they were as scared as she was.

The next few days were filled with tests of all kinds. There were X rays of her skull and CAT scans to determine if there was a tumor pressing against the optic nerve.

Finally, they got the verdict. No tumor. There was nothing they could do for her. The condition might worsen or it could stay the same.

Her mother gripped her arm with a hand that was icy cold. "We can send men to the moon. We can transplant hearts. Why can't we do something for her eyes!"

"We'll take her to San Francisco," her father said. "Somebody must be able to help her." Her father's voice broke, and he turned away.

Chelsea touched his shoulder. "Daddy, it's all right. My eyes aren't going to get any worse." She had never seen her father cry. She wanted to be brave. "It's not so bad. Honest."

Chelsea's mother held her daughter close. For a long time they just stood there saying nothing.

All the way home, the three of them sat in shocked silence. Chelsea felt numb, an icy numbness that filled her with dread. She kept saying over and over to herself, I can see better. I know it. I know it.

The only trouble was, she couldn't make herself believe what she was saying.

Three

CHELSEA'S sight wasn't getting any better. Everything seemed distorted. Doors looked wavy. She stumbled over things. She spent most of her time in her room, hoping no one would realize.

One morning she woke up earlier than usual. Sharon was still asleep in the other bed. Quietly, Chelsea sat down at the dressing table. She leaned forward to peer into the mirror as she did every morning now. It was like someone had drawn her reflection in disappearing ink. Little by little her face was disappearing from the mirror.

"It's getting worse, isn't it?"

Chelsea swung around to see Sharon leaning on her elbow. "Yes, but don't tell anybody."

Sharon sat up on the edge of her bed. "I know it's been rough on you."

"I didn't think you really cared."

"Of course I do! I've been leaving you alone

on purpose. Mom says you're going through a period of depression and withdrawal. She says you need to work this through alone. It seems kind of mean to me. But then ever since you were a little kid and would get hurt, you'd go off by yourself. Right?"

Chelsea nodded. "I guess I just feel sorry for myself sometimes."

"My gosh, you've got a right to. It just isn't fair."

"There are probably lots worse things, but right now I can't think of any."

"Little sister, I'll be going off to school soon, but if you ever need to talk, I'll listen." Sharon came over and gave Chelsea a hug. Then she glanced at the digital clock on the bedside table. "I'd better get going. I promised to meet Eric at eight. Did I tell you we have a gig lined up for the Labor Day weekend? And I get to sing with the group."

"That's super," Chelsea said, trying to sound bright and happy for her sister. "Do I get to come hear you?"

"You bet. You'll have front row seats."

Sharon hurriedly dressed. "Remember what I said about talking. See you later—I mean—bye now."

Chelsea put on old jeans and a T-shirt, then got out her diary. She hadn't entered a word in it since she'd been to see Dr. Myers.

Although she knew it by heart, she strained her eyes to read the last page.

Dear diary,

What a super day it's been. I got the greatest shot of Midnight. I caught him in mid-leap. I'll bet it can win a prize. And today, Kevin spoke to me. I mean, he really talked to me. It was only a minute, but he didn't treat me like a dumb little kid. . . .

What good would a diary do her now? She ripped out the pages, tore them up, and dropped the pieces into the wastebasket. Next she got out all her photos and albums. For a long time she brooded over the pictures, then slowly began to tear them up.

"Chelsea? Telephone," her mother called. "It's Tina."

Chelsea covered the torn pictures with her bedspread and opened her room door a crack. "I don't want to talk to anybody," she yelled.

Her mother came to the door and knocked. "Chelsea, honey, I know what you're going through. I understand your need to be alone, but you can't hide in this room forever."

"I'm not hiding. I just don't want to talk to anybody for a while. Okay?"

"It's not okay. You haven't been out of the house for weeks. You'll have to tell your friends some time. They're going to start wondering what's going on."

"I don't want their pity."

She heard her mother sigh. Chelsea knew she was being a pain, but she couldn't help it. Why can't everybody just leave me alone? she thought.

She went back to her bed, gathered the torn pictures into a pile, and shoved them into the wastebasket. She started to take the wastebasket out to the trash, then decided to throw away the negatives and the roll of partially used film in the camera, too.

Slipping out the back door, she carefully made her way around the house. She heard Billy and his friend Jeremy coming up the drive. Why did Billy have to bring someone to the house? Jeremy would tell his parents, and pretty soon everybody in Seaview would know she was going blind.

She hurriedly emptied the basket into the huge plastic garbage can. Photos, film, negatives—gone now. The sound was like a stab to her heart. It was the end of everything. Who ever heard of a blind photographer?

With Midnight at her heels she got back to her room without being seen. She stretched out on her bed and buried her face in the pillow. Is this what the world will look like soon? This darkness? Why? Why? Why me?

* * * * *

At lunchtime, her mother insisted that Chelsea come out to the kitchen and eat something.

To get from her room to the kitchen, Chelsea had to walk through the long living room. She was looking ahead so she wouldn't bump into the couch, when she stepped on something. Trying to avoid whatever it was, she stumbled and fell. She let out a yowl of hurt and anger as she realized what she'd fallen over. It was Billy's Monopoly game.

Her mother came running. "Chelsea! What happened?"

"It's Billy's darned game."

Her mother helped her to her feet. "Are you all right?"

"No, I'm not all right," she yelled. "Billy left that on the floor on purpose! I hate him. I hate all of you!"

As she ran out, she heard Billy calling, "Sis, I'm sorry. I forgot."

Chelsea hesitated at the back door. She felt awful for what she'd said. But she couldn't go back to apologize . . . not just yet, anyway.

"Leave her alone," she heard her mother say to Billy. "She's not really angry at us."

Chelsea closed the door behind her. Carefully, she made her way down the steps with Midnight at her heels. In the bright afternoon sun she found she could see better than in the house. She didn't have too much trouble getting to her favorite rock. Usually the dog raced ahead, but this time he stayed right beside her. He seemed to know she was upset.

When she had settled herself on a flat spot, Midnight put his head in her lap. He whined little soft cries that echoed the hurt inside her. She ruffled the fur behind his ears. "Midnight, what if I go totally blind? What if I never again see the moonlight on the waves? Or watch a sea gull soaring overhead? Or be able to see your funny face . . . ?" Hot tears welled up in her eyes, and she hugged her dog. "Oh, Midnight, what am I going to do . . . ?"

* * * * *

Chelsea was never sure how the news about her blindness got around. Maybe it was Jeremy. Or maybe someone had seen her fumbling her way down to the beach and guessed what was wrong.

The next day Tina came to the bedroom door and called, "Chelsea, I know you're there."

"Go away, Tina. I'm not feeling so well."

"You open this door, or I'm going to sit out

here in the hall until you do."

Chelsea knew Tina would do it, too. "Come on in. The door's not locked."

Chelsea was sitting in a chair facing the window. She didn't turn around. "I guess you heard, huh?"

Tina came up behind her and hugged her. "Gosh, Chelsea, why didn't you tell me about your eyes? I thought we were best friends."

"Because it's just temporary." Chelsea tried to sound unconcerned. "I was just having a little trouble with my eyes. It's getting better now." Her voice broke a little on the lie.

"Tell me the truth."

"I'm going blind," she blurted out. She bit her lip to keep from crying. "It's getting worse all the time."

"Oh, Chelsea. I—I didn't know." Tina came around and put her face close. "You can see me, can't you?"

"Yes, but not clearly. If I look directly at your face I can't see much. But if I look at the side of your head, I can."

"Gosh, I don't know what to say. I've never known a bli—" Tina stopped. "I'm sorry. I never knew anyone with an eye problem. Does it hurt?"

"No." At least not physically, she thought.

"Oh, Chelsea, what a crummy, lousy thing to happen."

"Yeah," Chelsea said in a trembly voice. "I won't be able to try out for the swim team this year. I guess we won't be able to do a lot of things any more."

"Pooh on the swim team. I won't try out for it either." Tina put her arms around Chelsea. "I'll help you as much as I can. Come on, I'm going to ask your mom and dad if you can go with us to the woods tomorrow."

"But I can't work. I'd cut off my hand."

"We could talk. It really gets boring out there without you."

"Okay, I guess it would be good to get out for a change."

As Chelsea started to get up, Tina grabbed her arm. "Here, let me help you."

"I can see okay if I take it slowly."

But as they walked out to the living room, Tina clutched Chelsea's arm. "Watch out for that chair! Be careful!"

Chelsea didn't know whether to be amused or upset. "Tina, I'm okay. Honest."

Her parents were watching television in the family room. "Mom, Dad, is it okay if I go with Tina tomorrow?"

"To the woods?" her dad asked. "No, I don't want you out there."

"But I wouldn't be working." She sure didn't need to earn money for photographic supplies anymore.

"It's too dangerous, Chelsea."

"You've both been hollering at me to get out of the house. Now, you won't let me go."

"Honey," her mother said, "you need to get more accustomed to getting around. Tomorrow, we'll go for a walk or a ride."

"Well, I have to go now," Tina said, "but I'll come over Saturday, early . . . about eight. We'll do something fun."

"No riding your bike," her father warned.

Chelsea sighed. Her father had always been protective of her. It's going to get lots worse, she thought.

"Let's go to the beach," Chelsea suggested. She hadn't dared try the long flight of stairs by herself. And she hadn't wanted to ask any of her family.

"Sure thing," Tina said.

Chelsea said goodnight to Tina, then went back into the family room. Billy was on the floor. Her mom and dad were in their recliners. Sharon was no doubt out with Eric. Chelsea sat down to watch TV, but it took too much concentration. She had trouble following the story.

During a commercial, her mother turned to Chelsea. "Honey, I've been thinking. I'm going to get things going before school starts."

"What things?" Chelsea asked.

"You'll get a battery of tests from

psychologists and specialists in the field. The sooner we get started the less school you'll miss."

Her father switched off the TV to the howls of Billy. "Go watch in the kitchen," her father told him. "Chelsea's sight is more important than a TV show."

"Chelsea's more important than *anything* else," he muttered.

"That's enough," their mother said. "Billy, I think you'd better get ready for bed."

"Why do I have to have more tests?" Chelsea asked after Billy left the room.

"We have to find out what you're capable of doing. Thank heavens I work in the school system. You'll have to have special classes. I know which teachers will give you the most help."

Chelsea didn't like the sound of it at all—special classes, special teachers. She'd be different, the poor little blind kid who's led around like a baby. She wanted to be just like everyone else.

"I don't see how she can get the proper help there," her father said. "Maybe she should go to one of those special schools for the blind."

Chelsea jumped up from the couch. "I'm not blind! I can still see some. It's not going to get any worse. I don't want to be with a bunch of blind kids. I'd hate it!"

"She's right, Steven. These days they try to mainstream handicapped children into the educational system."

"I'm not handicapped! You make it sound like I'm some kind of freak! I don't need any tests or special schools."

Chelsea's mother came over to her. "We'll talk about this when you're not upset."

"I don't want to talk about it tonight, tomorrow, or ever."

* * * * *

On Saturday, Chelsea was ready by eight o'clock.

By nine o'clock, she was getting anxious. Maybe she should call Tina. No, she was probably already on her way.

At ten she was sure Tina was avoiding her. After all, who wanted to drag around a blind person? That was as bad as getting stuck with your little brother. Chelsea headed back inside. Well, I don't need anybody, she told herself.

"Hey, Chelsea, wait up."

Tears stung Chelsea's eyes. Tina had come, after all.

Four

"CHELSEA?" Sharon called. "There's a letter for you."

Chelsea made her way from the family room to where her sister was going through the morning's mail. The only person she got letters from was a pen pal in Bangkok. "Does it have a Thailand postmark?"

"No. It was mailed right here in Seaview. Want me to read it to you?"

Chelsea snatched the letter from her sister's hand. "No!"

"Well, pardon me."

"I'm sorry I bit your head off, but it might be private."

Chelsea took the letter into her bedroom and opened the envelope. The card inside looked like an invitation or an announcement of some kind, but she just couldn't make out the letters. It was so frustrating not to be able to do the things she'd always done without a thought.

Later, when Tina came over, Chelsea asked her to read the card.

"Oh, good, you got one, too. It's an invitation to Kevin's party. I told you he'd ask us. It's on the beach, just like last year. What are you going to wear?"

"Nothing."

"Well, that'll get Kevin's attention!"

"No. I mean, I'm not going."

"Aw, come on. Is it because of your eyes?"

"You know it is."

"Look, I'll help you. Nobody even needs to know. I won't leave your side."

Chelsea tried to joke. "If I need a guide dog, I'd rather take Midnight."

"Please go. It won't be fun without you. Most of the other kids will be older."

"Do you think anybody knows about my eyes?"

"I haven't heard anyone talking about you."

Chelsea was torn. She really wanted to go. But she was afraid—afraid she'd do something embarrassing. "I don't know. . . ."

"I promise, if you aren't having a good time, we'll leave. Okay?"

"Oh . . . all right!"

"Super!" Tina gave her a bear hug. "We'll have a great time."

"When is it?"

"The party's at six o'clock, a week from

Friday. I can't wait!"

"I just hope it's not Friday the thirteenth."

* * * * *

Tina took that Friday off and came over in the afternoon to help Chelsea get ready. Tina put her blanket, towel, and beach bag on the bed. Then she held out her arms and turned around slowly. "How do you like my new outfit?"

The outlines of the red and white shorts and matching top were blurred, and Tina appeared wavy. Chelsea closed her eyes for a moment and tried again.

"You can see me, can't you?" Tina asked, and came closer.

"Of course. It's a cute outfit. Did you bring a bathing suit?"

"I have it on underneath. It's my old red bikini."

"I can't decide what to wear. I don't want to wear shorts. What do you think?"

Tina crossed to the huge closet that took up one wall. "My stuff's on the right," Chelsea said. "Sharon's is on the left."

"Boy, I don't know how you find anything in here."

"Don't you nag me, too. Mom and Sharon are always bawling me out."

"How about the jeans you got this spring? And this yellow top. Pale yellow looks terrific on you. And you can wear your yellow swimsuit underneath."

"I'm not going swimming," Chelsea said.

"Wear it anyhow. You might change your mind."

Chelsea doubted it. The thought of that huge ocean was scary. But to please Tina, she wore the suit.

Tina laid out the clothes on the bed. "Okay. Hair next."

Chelsea had shampooed her hair in the shower, and it was still damp. As Tina was blow-drying it, she sighed. "I sure wish I had hair like yours. You can wear it any way and it looks great."

"I'd trade for yours. All you have to do is wash your hair, shake your head, and you're ready to go."

"Yeah, me and Midnight."

Chelsea rummaged through the dresser drawers until she found a wide yellow ribbon. She started to put it on, but Tina took it from her. "Let me do that."

"Tina, I'm not helpless. I just can't see very clearly."

Chelsea sat at the dressing table to put on her eye makeup. She leaned as close to the mirror as possible. Her reflection was disappearing fast now. She'd read a science fiction story once where a man disappeared forever when he could no longer see his face in the mirror. She shivered and turned away.

"I think you'd better let me do that before you put out your eyes," Tina said softly.

With numb fingers, Chelsea let the pencil drop. "I don't think I want to go, after all."

"You can't let this get to you," Tina said as she sat down beside Chelsea. "You're the gutsiest person I know. Remember when you broke a bone in your foot? ~~Heck,~~ you were walking around on it in a week."

"This is different. I don't want everybody to know."

"I have an idea. I'll pretend I turned my ankle coming down the steps. I'll hang onto you, and everybody will think you're helping me walk."

"You're crazy."

"All geniuses are a little crazy."

* * * * *

When they were ready to leave, Chelsea went into the kitchen. "Mom? Do I look okay?"

"You look wonderful," her mother said. "You both do. You'll be the belles of the ball—beach ball, that is."

Chelsea and Tina groaned.

"I'm so glad you're finally getting out, Chelsea," her mother said, giving her daughter a kiss. "Your dad and I should be back from the movies about ten. Have fun, sweetheart."

"I'll try."

"I hope you took an old blanket."

"Yes, Mom. And I dug out an old beach towel."

Chelsea was glad her father wasn't home yet. He'd have had a dozen warnings.

As Chelsea went through the door, she had a moment of panic. She took a deep breath. Nobody knows about your eyes, she told herself. Just act natural.

Tina clutched Chelsea's arm in a death grip. "Remember, I'm supposed to have a sprained ankle," Tina said.

Chelsea heard Midnight's little cry of greeting. "You can't come with us this time. Mom?" she called. "Don't let Midnight follow us."

Her mother called the dog, and Chelsea and Tina started down the steep stairs to the beach. It was only a few minutes after six, but they could hear yells and laughter over the sound of the surf. And again, Chelsea wanted to run back to the safety of her room.

With Tina limping along, they made their way to the campfire. There were about twenty kids there, Chelsea guessed. Most of them were getting ready to go in swimming. Nobody spoke to Tina and Chelsea. Kevin hadn't even noticed their arrival. Tina hobbled over to a log and sat down.

Mrs. Gerrard came over immediately. "Tina, are you hurt?"

"Oh, I just twisted my ankle a bit. It's almost better."

Mrs. Gerrard turned to Chelsea. "My dear, I'm so glad you could make it. I can't tell you how sorry . . . " Her voice trailed off, and she made little clucking sounds of sympathy.

Chelsea stiffened. Kevin hadn't asked them. Mrs. Gerrard had just felt sorry for her. "It was nice of you to invite us," she said politely.

"We'll eat as soon as the sun sets," Mrs. Gerrard told them. "I'm sure you won't be going in swimming." She shook her head sadly. "What heartache for your mother. You tell her if there's anything I can do. . . ." Again her voice trailed off into an embarrassed silence.

Chelsea plunked down beside Tina. "I thought you said nobody knew about my eyes. Boy, to hear her, you'd think I was ready to sell pencils on the street corner!"

"Forget about her. Let's go swimming."

"You go on. I'm not up to it. I'll wait here."

"Sure you don't mind?" Chelsea shook her head. Tina peeled off her clothes and set them on the log. "Watch my stuff. I'll just go for a few minutes."

"Sure."

"Positive you don't mind?"

"Go! I'm fine."

Chelsea watched Mrs. Gerrard and some other women who were busy bringing boxes of things down from the house. They set up folding tables loaded with food.

The evening was unusually warm with no wind. A butterscotch-pink glow settled over the cliffs, sand dunes, and driftwood left from the last storm. Chelsea turned her head so she could see the setting sun out of the sides of her eyes. The orange-rose sky was so beautiful it almost hurt. She sat there for a long time trying to impress the sight on her mind. I never want to forget what this looks like, she thought.

Several kids came running up, laughing and kicking sand. One of the girls smiled at Chelsea and said hi.

Chelsea nodded. "Is the water warm?"

"Brr. Everybody says I'll get used to this cold water. But I don't believe it." The girl wrapped her blanket around her shoulders. "I'm Julie."

"Hi. I'm—"

But before Chelsea could finish, the rest of the kids came back. Everyone was laughing or yelling or horsing around. Someone turned on a radio. A lot of the kids started dancing.

"Where's the food?"

"I'm thirsty. Kev, you have any sodas?"

Chelsea watched a blurred Kevin take cans of pop from a large camp cooler. He's so easy with people, she thought. She'd always thought he was the best-looking guy she knew. He was six foot three and played forward on the basketball team. He had brown eyes and blond hair. His brows and lashes were so dark, Chelsea and Tina had speculated about whether he bleached his hair.

Tina was laughing at Mickey Calhoun. At least she was having a good time.

Chelsea noticed Mrs. Gerrard whisper to Kevin, then he turned to look at Chelsea. Quickly, she bent over and pretended to be very busy tying her shoelace. She didn't look up until she saw his bare feet in front of her.

"Hi, Chelsea. Have a soda." He was holding a can. "Is cola okay?"

"It's fine. Thanks." She took the icy can and held it to her hot face.

He stood in embarrassed silence for a moment, then said, "How did that picture come out of me and your mutt licking my face?"

"I haven't had the film developed yet." She didn't want to tell him she'd thrown everything away.

"I—uh—heard about—your eyes. I'm sure—"

Another kid came up and stuck his face close to Chelsea's. "Gee, you don't look like you're blind."

"So, how am I supposed to look?" Chelsea snapped.

"Hey, Chelsea," a boy called, "did you know your shoes don't match?"

Instinctively, she looked down to check her feet. Some of the kids laughed. Chelsea tried to laugh, too.

Nobody else teased her, but Chelsea could hear whispering and was sure people were talking about her. She wished she could sink right through the sand. She wished she hadn't come.

She decided to tell Tina she wanted to leave, but Tina was dancing with Mickey. She doubted if Tina had even heard the kids' teasing. Chelsea was glad Tina was having fun. It wasn't every day that an older kid paid attention to a freshman. She didn't want to spoil the party for her friend.

After a while the girl Julie came over. "Can I get you something to eat?" she asked.

The very thought of food made Chelsea sick. "Thanks, but I'm going to go on home. I'm not feeling too well. Would you mind telling Mrs. Gerrard and Tina Webb that I've gone home? Tina's the cute dark-haired girl in the red and white outfit."

"Sure, but can you make it by yourself?"

"No problem. I could go home from here blindfolded—I know the way."

But instead of going home, Chelsea walked down the beach toward the cove. There was still a little twilight left, so she decided to swim for a while. She could still do anything anybody else could do. Who needed them anyway?

She slipped off her jeans, shirt, and shoes and headed toward the water. She had played in the ocean since she was a tiny girl, but now it seemed huge and unfamiliar. I'll show them I'm not a helpless baby, she thought as she waded into the water. The shock of the cold almost made her change her mind, but she was determined. Hadn't Tina said she had guts?

Chelsea swam out past the breakers. The water felt warmer now, and she floated on her back. The sky was black. She couldn't see any stars. Will I ever see the stars again? she wondered. Oh, how I hate having everybody know about my eyes. Nobody will ever treat me the same again. Nothing will ever be the way it was. She began to swim, furiously trying to rid herself of the anger inside her.

Feeling a change in the tide, she started to swim toward shore. But then she heard the crash of breakers against rocks and knew she must have drifted toward the cove. It was stupid to have come out alone, but she was a strong swimmer. There was nothing to worry about. She just had to head for shore. But the currents here were strong, and they came from all directions. Suddenly, she felt as if she were caught in a whirlpool, sucking her under. Water closed over her head, filling her eyes and mouth. She came up choking and gasping. She'd never been afraid in the water before, but now she panicked. Her heart thundered in her chest. She flailed her arms wildly, trying to pull away from the swirling current.

Finally, her father's words came to her. *If you ever have trouble with currents or riptides, keep calm, and swim parallel to the shore, not toward it.*

But which way? Away from the crash of waves against the rocks, she thought. Using all her strength she swam free of the terrible current and then made for shore.

She sank onto the sand exhausted. I'm safe, she thought. I made it. I made it. She wasn't sure how long she lay there gasping for breath. After a bit she got to her feet and tried to figure out where she was. But she was totally disoriented. It was so dark. She couldn't see anything on the beach. Were her clothes to the left or to the right?

She held her breath and listened. But she

couldn't hear any sounds except the waves breaking on the shore. She turned to the left and stumbled over a log. In an icy sweat now, she ran back and forth, stumbling, falling over driftwood and rocks.

"Help!" she cried. "Someone please help me!"

The only answer was the scream of a seagull and the sound of the surf.

Shivering with cold and fear, she sank to her knees in the damp sand. "Mom! Daddy!"

On hands and knees, she crawled as far away from the water as she could get. She huddled there trembling, peering into the frightening blackness. When she was little she'd been afraid of the dark. Monsters and terrible things hid in the dark bedroom. And now they were here. They had followed her from her childhood nightmares. "Please, God, help me," she whispered.

"Chelseeee . . . ?"

She stood up. Was that the cry of a bird?

Then she heard Midnight's familiar yip. "Here!" she shouted. "Over here!"

Midnight almost knocked her over trying to lick her face. "Down boy," she said, laughing and crying at the same time.

Tina rushed up. "Oh, thank heavens, it's you." She gave Chelsea a huge bear hug, then cried, "Are you crazy? I almost died when I found you weren't at the house! What are you doing way down here by yourself? I've never been so afraid. . . ."

"Me, either," Chelsea said. "How'd you find me?"

"Your dog. I think he knew you were in trouble. I just followed him. He found your clothes. Then I was really scared."

Still shaking, Chelsea put on her jeans, shirt, and sweater.

"Why'd you do it?" Tina asked.

"I know it was stupid, but I just had to prove I wasn't helpless. Don't tell my dad. He'd have a heart attack or something."

"I won't tell if you promise you won't go off alone that way again. I didn't even know you'd left." Then Tina squealed, "Guess what? Oh, Chelsea, Mickey asked me if I'd like to go skating next Saturday. Can you believe it?"

And suddenly Chelsea felt cold again. And alone.

Five

A few weeks before school started Chelsea had to go through dozens of tests with psychologists and specialists in spatial modality and other big words she didn't understand. Her mother had arranged for her to have an early IEP meeting, Individualized Educational Program. That meant her doctor, the psychologists, counselors, teachers, and her parents all got together to discuss goals for her.

Chelsea sat there only half listening to everybody talk about her as if she were a plate of spaghetti. She resented them for telling her what she ought to be able to accomplish. Why should she learn braille and how to use a cane or any of the other aids for the blind? She could still see enough to get around. The only blind person she'd ever known was a pathetic old man who used to shuffle through the park. All the kids had avoided him as if he had some horrible disease. I won't be like him, she thought. I won't! Nobody's going to pity me.

Finally, they asked for her opinion.

"I want to go to regular classes."

"I'm afraid that's impossible," the principal said. "However, you can attend English and history with the rest of your class. Someone will be assigned to assist you."

"May I have my friend Tina help me?"

"It doesn't always work out to have best friends together. But we can certainly try it and see."

"How will she do her math?" her father asked. He was a whiz at math and had made all his kids learn their multiplication tables in the second grade.

"She will have to learn Nemeth Code for mathematics. She'll also use talking calculators and computers."

He turned back to Chelsea. "For most of the day you'll be in a special resource room for visually handicapped students. We're extremely proud of it. One of our Seaview service organizations has donated money for the very latest equipment. Mr. Lewis will be your teacher. Anything to add, John?"

"Hi, Chelsea," her new teacher said. "I know it all seems very bewildering right now. If you have any problems, we can solve them. Okay?"

Chelsea nodded sullenly. I have only one

problem, she thought, and nobody can solve it. I'm going blind.

* * * * *

On the first day of school, Chelsea's entire family helped her get ready. Billy was tying her shoes. Her mother was brushing her hair. Sharon was applying her lip gloss. "You'd think I was being presented to the Queen of England," Chelsea said.

"Stop talking," her sister told her. "This stuff will be all over your face."

Chelsea's dad was wearing out the carpet. "I don't like this," he said for the dozenth time. "Madelyn, I think you should stay with her today."

"Steven, you wanted me to stay with the children when they started the first grade. Chelsea's perfectly capable of taking care of herself. Anyway, I'll be right there on campus if she needs me."

"Well, I'll be there to pick you up after school," he said.

"Moth—er!" He was really making her feel like a first grader.

"Steven, will you stop worrying," her mother told him. "Tina has promised to meet Chelsea at lunchtime and to bring her home after school."

Chelsea had had to argue for an hour to get her father to agree to let her walk to school with Tina. "Daddy, I'll get along fine if you'll just leave me alone. You're all making me nervous."

"Madelyn, I still think you should have taken a year off work to tutor her," he went on. "She's going to—"

Chelsea was saved by the door chimes. "That'll be Tina," she said, and picked up her canvas bag. "Do I look okay?"

Everyone assured her she looked wonderful, but she wished she could really tell for herself. She kissed everybody except Billy who stuck out his tongue. "I saw that," she said.

"Yeah, I knew you were just pretending so you'd get your own way."

"Sure. It's a ton of fun having everybody treat you like you're a baby."

"Billy, knock it off," Sharon said. "The poor kid's got enough problems."

They all followed her to the door. As Chelsea stepped onto the porch, she wanted to turn around, run to her room and hide. From now on, she'd be "that blind kid." Nothing would ever be the same again. Heart pounding, with a dry throat and sweaty hands, she waved to her family.

"Come on, Tina, let's go before I chicken out."

* * * * *

When Tina left her at the open door of the resource room, Chelsea stood frozen. I don't want to do this, she thought. I don't want to go in there.

"Chelsea, good morning." Mr. Lewis came right over to her. "Come in and meet the rest of the class."

The room seemed huge. Mr. Lewis led her over to a large round table and introduced her to seven kids, all legally blind. They'd all been in the class the year before. One boy had cerebral palsy and was in a wheelchair. Another was deaf. They were friendly, laughing and joking together. She supposed they were all nice enough, but she hated the idea of being with blind kids.

"We're pretty informal here, Chelsea. Everybody calls me John. And this is Betty Weintraub. She's a teacher's aide. She'll show you around."

As they toured the large room, Betty pointed out all the equipment. There were Perkins Braillers, a VersaBraille System, a closed circuit TV with a scanner for partially sighted students, and several Opticons—optical to tactile converters. There were special copying machines and a soundproof room for listening and dictating to tapes.

How am I going to learn to use all this stuff and keep up with my homework, too? Chelsea wondered.

"Over here is the cupboard for games," Betty said. "We have everything from Scrabble to beep balls."

"Beep balls?"

"Sure, so you can hear the ball. We use lots of beepers. To the right of that are the talking computers. Do you know how to type?"

"Some, but I'm not very fast. And we have a computer at home. It doesn't talk, though."

"We have talking books, too." Betty led Chelsea over by the windows. "We have a large library . . . for school and for fun."

A talking book will probably put me to sleep, Chelsea thought.

Betty took Chelsea to a large table with a typewriter, a braillewriter, and a TV. "This is your work area. Tomorrow, we'll work on sensitizing. You'll learn to identify things by touch, by their textures and shapes."

As Chelsea pulled out the chair and sat down, Betty spoke to someone who had just come up. "Hi, Marty, come meet Chelsea Moore."

As the boy came closer, Chelsea could make out that Marty was tall, lean, and athletic-looking, like a tennis player.

"Chelsea, this is Marty Talbot, a student

aide. He'll be showing you how to use some of this equipment."

"Hi, Chelsea. Glad to meet you," he said. His voice was deep and clear, like a radio announcer.

Chelsea gave him a grudging hello.

Betty went off to help one of the other kids. "Let's start off with the braillewriter," Marty said, and pulled up another chair.

"Braille is a system of reading by touch using an arrangement of dots." He picked up a card and held it out. "Run your fingers over the card. Can you feel the raised dots?"

Chelsea nodded.

"Are you having trouble finding them?" he asked.

"My hands are still kind of rough from picking ferns, but I can feel the bumps. They don't feel like letters, though. It just feels like heavy paper someone's stuck pins through."

"Each group of dots represents letters. It takes a while to learn. There are so many new techniques now that a lot of blind people don't want to learn braille."

"I'm not *blind!* I can see just fine."

"Chelsea, I've read your file. You can just barely see me, can't you?"

"Yes," she admitted. "But I don't need this dumb braille stuff. Who can make any sense out of a bunch of dots? Anyway, I'm not going to need it. I can see better every day. I don't know what I'm doing here in this place."

" 'This place' has been like going to heaven for me," Marty said. "My folks even moved here temporarily so I could learn to use all this great equipment."

"Why? Are you going to be a resource teacher like Mr. Lewis?"

"No. I came here because I'm blind."

Stunned, Chelsea leaned forward, trying to see Marty's eyes. He must be making a sick joke, she thought. "I don't believe it. You get around too easily. And you said you'd read my file."

"I did . . . in braille. I've been blind all my life."

Chelsea felt like a jerk. "I'm sorry."

"That's okay. I get kind of a kick out of it when I fool people."

She couldn't really see his smile, but she could hear it in his voice. As he explained some of the machines, he was patient when she didn't understand how they worked.

"You must have been using this equipment for ages to know so much about it," she told him.

"Just a year. At first, it seemed really scary. I probably learned fast because I was just so glad I could come here. I'd like to be a computer programmer."

A computer programmer? Boy, he sure had some wild dreams. "Why not an airline pilot?" she asked, a bit sarcastically.

He laughed. "I'm too tall."

It was hard not to like the guy. Before she knew it, it was time for lunch.

"Want me to show you the way to the cafeteria?" Marty asked. "It's a little tricky the first couple of times."

"Thanks," Chelsea said quickly. "A friend's meeting me." The last thing she wanted was to be identified with "blind kids."

"Oh . . . sure. See you tomorrow."

Chelsea was certain he had realized she hadn't wanted to go to the cafeteria with him—and why. "Marty? Thanks, though. And thanks for your help. Maybe it won't be so bad, after all."

Chelsea gathered up her things and waited outside for Tina. Mr. Lewis and the other kids came out.

"Want to come along with us?" John asked her.

"Thanks, but I'm waiting for a friend."

After what seemed like ages, Chelsea was beginning to think that Tina had forgotten her. "But Tina's always late," she told herself. "Surely, she wouldn't forget me." Her stomach began to churn. It was one thing to walk around familiar places, but she had no idea how to find her way to the cafeteria or to her mother's office. She started to go back inside when Betty came out.

"Chelsea, you're not back already?"

"I never left. I'm not hungry. I'll just wait inside."

"I'm sorry, but I have to lock up. Come on, I'll show you how to get to the cafeteria. At least you can sit down there."

"I guess my friend must have forgotten me."

"The first day of school is always hard. She probably got lost," Betty said, locking the door of the resource room. "Now, take my right arm just above the elbow. Don't ever let anyone grab your arm and try to steer you."

On the way, Betty described the buildings they passed. "Notice we're on grass now instead of the sidewalk. Listen to sounds. Hear the leaves in the maples? The children on the playground? The cars out in the street?"

It was all just a jumble of sounds. "Sure," Chelsea said, cupping her hand to her ear. "What's that! A worm inching his way through the dirt?"

Betty ignored her smart remark. "Try to remember every turn. Get used to making mental maps."

"You sound as if you think I'll go totally blind. Well, I won't!"

"I always figure it's best to plan for the worst and hope for the best," Betty said calmly as if Chelsea hadn't spoken sharply. "It won't hurt to learn as much as you can about getting around."

Chelsea supposed that made sense. She paid close attention as Betty talked.

"We're passing the gym now—on your right. Make a habit of listening for echoes. They bounce sharply off brick, not so much off glass. And off soft surfaces, the echo is muffled. After a while you'll even be able to tell distances by how long it takes an echo to return."

Chelsea shook her head. "I'll never learn all that."

"You'll be surprised. Well, here we are. Hear the sounds inside?"

Chelsea heard the jumbled sounds of talking, laughing, and the clatter of dishes.

"Now, notice the smells?" Betty told her. "You can always tell when you're near the cafeteria at lunchtime."

Chelsea sniffed deeply. She'd never noticed before how many different sounds and smells there were.

As they went inside, Betty said, "The food line's to your right. The trays and silverware are first."

As they went through the line, Betty named

off the food. "It's pizza, carrot and celery sticks, fruit cocktail, and brownies. There's milk to drink. Is that okay?"

"Fine." Except for the fruit cocktail, she could eat everything with her fingers . . . no chance of accidents.

"Do you want to sit with the rest of the class?" Betty asked.

Chelsea started to answer, when Tina came hurrying over. "Hey, Chelsea. I'm sorry. I was just coming to get you when I bumped into Mickey." She whispered excitedly, "I think he's really starting to like me. Come on over to my table and meet some new kids in my math and science classes."

Chelsea hesitated.

"Go ahead," Betty said. "I'll be here if you need help getting back to the resource room."

"That's okay," Tina said. "I'll see that she gets back."

Tina grabbed Chelsea's tray, and Chelsea followed her to a large table in the corner. She heard a lot of laughing and chattering.

"Here, take my place," Tina told her. "I'll get another chair. Watch it! Alicia, would you move over a bit. Hey, everybody, this is my friend, Chelsea. And this is Marsha and Amy and Jan." As Tina introduced everyone, she talked too fast and her voice was too high. She sounded embarrassed.

The girls at the table said hi. One girl said, "I didn't see you in any of my classes. Who's your homeroom teacher?"

"Mr. Lewis."

"Oh, yeah. He's the one with all those—ouch!" she said, as if someone had kicked her to keep quiet.

Nobody said anything. They had been laughing and talking until Chelsea arrived. Now they were silent. Chelsea took a bite of pizza, but it tasted like catsup-covered cardboard. She picked up her spoon and dropped it. It clattered on the tray.

"Here, let me help," Tina said, and put the spoon in her hand.

"Maybe you'd like to feed me, too!"

As Chelsea jumped up, she tipped over her milk. "I'm sorry! I'm sorry!" Almost in tears now, she pushed back her chair. It fell over. In her hurry to leave, she bumped into the next table. "I'm sorry!" she cried.

"Wait up, Chelsea," Tina called.

Chelsea didn't answer. She rushed toward the light of the open door. Outside, she leaned against the wall of the building.

Tina came hurrying up to her. "Chelsea, come on back. I explained to everyone about—you know."

"It's okay." Chelsea's throat was tight from trying to keep from crying. "Tina, I want to be alone right now. I'll just wait here for the rest of my class. Okay?"

"Sure, I guess so." Tina touched her arm. "But I'll pick you up for English class. I promise I won't be late."

Chelsea nodded. She knew Tina stood there for a moment, before going back inside.

As soon as she was sure she was alone, the tears welled up in her eyes. She'd made such a fool of herself.

"Are you okay?"

Chelsea recognized Marty's voice. She brushed her eyes with her sleeve. "Oh, I'm just great. I made a real jerk of myself in there."

"You weren't a jerk. We've all been through the same thing. You should have seen me the first time I ordered a milkshake. I nearly stuck the straw up my nose."

Chelsea smiled feebly. "I guess you heard me crashing into things. I don't know how many chairs I knocked over."

"We heard the commotion. When Betty said you'd left the cafeteria, I offered to see if you were okay."

"I'll never go back in there again. I'll starve first."

"Give your friends time to get used to it. It's hard for sighted people to deal with blindness."

"I'm not—"

"I know, I know." He laughed. "You're not blind."

She had to laugh at herself, too. "I guess it's pretty stupid to keep saying I'm not blind when I bump into tables and knock over milk."

"It'll get better," he said. "I promise."

"Can you give me a written guarantee?"

"Sure. But it will have to be in braille."

This time she really smiled. "What a sneaky way to make me learn those dumb dots."

Six

TINA came hurrying up to the resource room where Chelsea was waiting. "I made it," Tina said, all out of breath. "Wouldn't you know my science class is clear across campus?"

Tina started to take Chelsea's arm. "No, let me take yours," Chelsea said. "And walk just a little ahead of me."

They took off at a fast walk. "Hey, Chelsea, I'm sorry about what happened at the cafeteria."

"It's okay." She grinned. "Except I'm starving."

"I have a roll of mints, if that'll help."

They stopped for a minute while Tina opened a package and gave Chelsea one of the candies. "Here, keep it," Tina said. "Just don't let Bolton see it. I hear she's a bear about rules."

"I'm really nervous about this class," Chelsea said.

"Don't worry. I'll be there with you."

By the time they got to Mrs. Bolton's room, the teacher was telling the class what she expected of them. "I will not tolerate rude behavior." She stopped as Chelsea and Tina stepped into the room, then pointedly added, "And arriving late to this class will result in detention. Don't just stand there, girls. Find a seat."

What a great way to start out, Chelsea thought. She knew everyone was staring at them. Tina grabbed her arm and pulled her forward. "Come on, there are a couple of seats in the back," she whispered.

"I expect you to always bring your books, to be prepared, to listen to me, and to refrain from talking in class," Mrs. Bolton went on.

Everything was a blur to Chelsea as Tina practically dragged her to the back of the room. Chelsea heard a few titters and wished she were safely back in the resource room.

"Right here," Tina said, just as Chelsea tripped over something.

Chelsea tried to catch her balance, but hit against the arm of a chair. "I'm sorry," she said.

"In the future," the teacher said, "do not leave books lying in the aisle."

I love books, Chelsea thought as she was finding a seat. She remembered that when she was about nine, she had planned to read every book in the library. It had seemed to take forever just to get through the *A's*. Betty had told her that all her literature assignments would be on tape. It was going to take her much longer to do homework now.

Chelsea brought her attention back to English class. She knew she was going to have to really concentrate on listening and remembering everything she heard. She tried to jot down notes, but she couldn't see if she was staying on the lines.

"We will cover the short story," Mrs. Bolton was saying, "the novel, poetry, and drama. This will be your assignment for tomorrow."

Chelsea heard the squeak of chalk and knew the teacher was writing on the board. "Get that for me," she whispered to Tina.

"Perhaps some of you didn't hear me earlier," the teacher said quietly. "There will be no whispering in this class."

Chelsea was embarrassed and missed the next few things that the teacher told them. The kids in the resource room had said that some teachers didn't like to have kids with special problems in their classes. Maybe Mrs. Bolton was like that.

After class, Chelsea said to Tina, "I want to ask Mrs. Bolton something."

As Tina led her to the teacher's desk some

of their friends came up with words of encouragement and offers of help.

"Thanks, guys," Chelsea said, trying to joke. "Just don't leave your legs sticking out in the aisle."

The others left, and Chelsea spoke up, "Mrs. Bolton, may I talk to you for a minute?"

"Yes. What is it, girls?"

Chelsea took a deep breath. "I'm sorry we were late."

"I understand and sympathize with your situation—Chelsea, isn't it?"

Chelsea nodded.

"But do you really think you're ready for mainstreaming? You could wait until next year."

"No, please, Mrs. Bolton. I want to be with my friends. And literature's my favorite subject."

"You have to realize that there just isn't time to give you special attention."

"I know. I was just thinking. If I could bring my tape recorder to class, I think I could keep up."

"Oh, I don't know," Mrs. Bolton said doubtfully. "Frankly, I don't like to have my words monitored."

"Please?" There was a long pause. Chelsea wished she could see the teacher's face. "I'll try really hard."

"All right. Your mother and John Lewis talked to me about you. They think you can handle this class. And you think you can, so—bring your tape recorder. We'll see how it works out."

"Thank you," Chelsea said. "You won't be sorry." *I hope,* she added under her breath.

Outside, Tina breathed a deep sigh. "I'm going to hate this class."

"I just hope I don't leave a music tape in the recorder by accident and punch the wrong button."

* * * * *

Chelsea's mother, with Billy's help, put the finishing touches on the chocolate marble cake. "How does it look?" Chelsea asked.

"It's a bit lopsided. But I'm sure Sharon will like it."

Chelsea didn't know why they were making all this fuss about Sharon going away to college. She had seen very little of her sister since Labor Day when Sharon had made her debut as a singer with Eric's band. Now she acted like she was a big star or something.

"Where's that dessert?" her father called from the dining room.

Chelsea's mother picked up the cake. "Coming," she said. "Billy, you bring the ice cream. Chelsea, get some extra spoons and forks."

Chelsea followed slowly. She had to feel her way now. She could see shapes and large objects, but the last few weeks, her sight had deteriorated even more.

Sharon cut the cake and everyone sang "For She's a Jolly Good Fellow." Then Sharon opened her presents—a blue sweater from her mom, a portable typewriter from her dad, a poster of her favorite rock star from Billy . . . and from Chelsea, a pair of earrings that her mom picked out for Sharon's pierced ears.

Chelsea wasn't listening to the others talking about college. She was thinking about what had happened at school. Mr. Lewis had told her that a special orientation and mobility instructor was coming to teach her to use a cane. A cane! Chelsea picked at her cake, pushing the pieces around the plate.

"What's the matter, Chelsea?" her mother asked. "Are you coming down with a cold?"

Chelsea shook her head.

"Have a bad day at school?" her father asked.

"They're all bad," Chelsea muttered.

"Do you have to sulk on my last night at home?" Sharon wanted to know. "All you ever think about is yourself."

Chelsea stood up. She gripped the back of

her chair to still the angry trembling of her hands. "Mother, may I be excused?"

"Watch her get out of helping with the dishes," Billy said.

"I'm just going outside for some fresh air."

"Chelsea, it's cold out there," her father said. "You put on a jacket."

As she went into the kitchen, she heard her mother whisper, "I wish all of you would be more patient and understanding. She's going through a rough time now."

"Well, it's not easy on us either, Mom. We all have—"

Chelsea closed the back door on Sharon's words. She knew she was making life miserable for them. She knew it, but she couldn't seem to help it. She was so afraid . . . .

She sat down on the step. She could hear the ocean and smell the ocean, but she could no longer see it or even be sure of the direction except by sound. Midnight came up and nuzzled her hand, then settled down by her feet. "At least you're not mad at me," she whispered.

In a few minutes her mother came outside and sat down beside her. Neither of them said anything for a bit. Then her mother sighed. "Honey, I'd give anything if I could trade eyes with you. But I can't."

Chelsea didn't answer.

"I don't know what to say to you. I'm a counselor. I've helped hundreds of kids, yet I can't find the words to help you get through this."

Chelsea felt her mother's arm around her shoulder, and she tensed.

"You know, you have every right to be angry and hurt," her mother said quietly. "It's normal." She hesitated a moment as if expecting Chelsea to say something. When she didn't, her mother asked, "Now, what happened today? Do you want to talk about it?"

"Mom, they're going to make me use a cane," Chelsea blurted out. "Do I have to? Can't you do something about it? I might just as well have a big sign on my back that says I'M BLIND. PITY POOR CHELSEA."

"It's the safest way to get around on your own. Almost every blind person uses a cane."

"Marty Talbot doesn't. He's a student aide, and you should see him get around without a cane. I didn't even realize he was blind the first time I met him."

"I'm Marty's counselor. It's different for him. He's congenitally blind. He's had sixteen years to get used to getting around on his own."

"I suppose he told you how lousy I'm doing in school."

"We discussed *his* problems."

"I didn't think he had any." Chelsea sighed, some of the anger gone now. "I don't know how he can be so cheerful all the time."

"He's learned to cope—just as you're going to have to do. Honey, you have a choice. You can sit around the house and cry about what's happened to you."

"I don't cry!"

"And all you'll accomplish is wearing out the furniture," her mother went on calmly. "Or you can take advantage of everything the school has to offer. Learn to use braille, a cane, and all the special equipment. Learn to function on your own—and be a success. It's your choice."

"Some choice," Chelsea mumbled.

"Life's not easy. But you can't change what's happened. You have to go forward."

Easy for her to say, Chelsea thought. Just doing the simplest thing was so darned frustrating. "Mom, I don't know if I can do it. Getting ready for school now takes forever. I spill half my food. I keep losing the toothpaste off my brush. I don't know how to do anything. Mom, it's so hard. . . ."

"Oh, sweetheart." Her mother pulled her close. Chelsea could feel tears on her mother's cheeks. "You can do it. I know you can. It'll be easier when the counselor from the Rehab

Center comes to teach you how to do some of these things."

Chelsea gave a deep, quivering sigh. "I'll try, Mom. But please don't get mad at me if I can't."

"How could I ever be mad at you? I love you. We all love you. All we ask is that you do your best."

"Okay, I'll try," Chelsea said.

"Maybe we should go back inside now. I'm getting cold."

Chelsea realized her mother was shivering in the damp night air. "I'm sorry I spoiled the party. You know, Mom, I really am going to miss Sharon."

* * * * *

One afternoon of the following week, the lady from the Rehabilitation Center came to the house to help Chelsea.

They started with Chelsea's room. "The key to taking care of yourself is organization," Mrs. Andrews said. "You have to learn to keep everything in its place."

Chelsea could hear the closet slide open. She was embarrassed and wished she had tried to straighten out her things while she could still see what she was doing.

Mrs. Andrews showed her how to put color-matched clothes together. "You can identify your clothes by texture, by collars, and by sleeves. To tell colors apart mark your things with aluminum braille tags or safety pins. Sew a button or yarn loop on to show you which is the front or back."

Next they went in to the kitchen. "I'm glad to see you have a microwave oven. They're much safer. Mrs. Moore, you can mark the stove dials and the temperature settings on the washer and dryer with a daub of glue. There are commercial products you can buy, but the glue works. Chelsea, you'll need to learn the sizes and shapes of foods and other household supplies. Learn how each container sounds and smells."

"What about eating?" her mother asked. "Chelsea's losing weight because she finds it so difficult to eat."

Chelsea turned toward her mother, surprised. "I didn't think anyone had noticed."

"For some people it helps if you arrange the food as if the plate is a clock. Put the meat at six o'clock, because it's easier to cut meat when it's directly in front of you. Put the vegetable at twelve, potatoes at three—just always use the same system. A plate with raised edges will help, too."

After a while Chelsea's head was spinning with all the things she had to learn—things she'd always taken for granted like dialing a phone, threading a needle, peeling potatoes, or putting on makeup.

"Any questions, Chelsea?"

"Yes. Will you please tell me how to keep the darned toothpaste on my brush. It always ends up a yucky mess in the sink."

"Simple. Just squeeze a little into the palm of one hand, then dip the brush in it. That's one way, at least."

Chelsea laughed. "I wish everything was that easy. I'll never get the hang of all this."

"It just takes time and patience—on your part as well as your family's. Don't be afraid to ask them questions. Train yourself to listen carefully, and ask yourself, 'What was that sound?' Then ask someone to tell you if you're right or wrong.

"Etch a map of the house in your mind," Mrs. Andrews continued. "I can't stress too strongly how important it is to try to picture everything in your mind. If you don't you may lose the ability to visualize."

That thought was terrifying. What if I forget what Mom and Dad look like? What if I can't remember what I look like?

After Mrs. Andrews left, Chelsea spent the rest of the day walking through the house trying to visualize every piece of furniture, every knickknack or picture. When she was tired she whistled for Midnight, who was never very far from her. "Come here, you," she said to the dog. "Let me look at you. I don't ever want to forget that funny little face."

* * * * *

Chelsea had no more than stepped into the resource room the next day when Marty called, "Chelsea, the O and M teacher will be here in a few minutes to start your cane training."

"Ugh," she said. "I'm going to hate this."

"Probably. But why not do things the easiest way—even if that means using a cane or learning braille?"

"That's what my mom said. But who listens to moms?"

"Once in a while they're right."

"Marty, how did you know it was me at the door? You sure must have super hearing."

"No, I don't. I've just worked hard at it. People always think that if you're blind your other senses are automatically stronger. It's not true. I just concentrate harder and practice using all my other senses."

"You mean I'll really be able to do all the things you do?"

"Maybe not everything. Remember, I've been doing this all my life. And I was lucky.

My parents let me explore and get hurt. You wouldn't believe all the times I've broken my nose or my toes."

"I'll probably break my silly neck trying to use a cane." In a low voice, almost to herself, she said. "Marty, I'm scared."

"I know. If I can help, just holler. Everything new is scary. After school today, I have to learn to dance. Man, I really dread it, but my mom says everybody should know how to dance."

"If you need to practice, come on over to my house some time. I can help with that." As soon as the words were out of her mouth, she regretted them. Marty seemed really nice, but she didn't want Tina and her other friends to see her with him.

"Well, I guess I'd better turn in my homework before the instructor gets here," she said.

* * * * *

The aluminum cane had a metal tip and was covered with reflective white tape. It was much longer than Chelsea had expected. She'd been imagining a wooden cane like Grandad Moore used.

Mrs. Harrison, the orientation and mobility instructor, explained the use of the long cane.

"It's like a probe so you can detect obstacles before you come to them. It can help you locate stairs and curbs."

Chelsea learned to hold the cane properly, to tap it, to locate door handles, to find something she had dropped.

Well, she thought after the first session, I'll use the darned thing at home, but I'll never use it to get to classes or out where people can see me. No way.

Seven

"MOM, will you take me to the mall this morning?" Chelsea asked at breakfast one Saturday. "I want to buy an angora sweater with my last fern-picking check. Tina said Teen Alley is having a sale."

"Oh, honey, I'm sorry. I promised to teach a parenting class. Then I have to go to the battered children clinic. If I get back in time this afternoon, maybe we can go. Or better still, why don't you call Tina?"

"I already did," Chelsea said. "She has to work all day. Daddy, do you have time?"

"I have an appointment at the office. And I'm already late. Billy," her father asked, "why don't you take your sister over to the mall?"

"Dad, I'm supposed to meet Jeremy this morning. How come I'm the one who always has to—"

"Forget it! Just forget it," Chelsea yelled. As she rushed out of the room, she cracked her shin against the china cabinet. She heard the dishes rattle, but she didn't care if they all broke.

Her mother followed her to the bedroom. "Chelsea, you can't expect everyone to just drop what they're doing."

Chelsea stopped and turned toward her mother. "I don't. But every time I ask, it's 'Not now. Maybe later.' I hate it. I hate asking for help."

"Of course you hate it. Anyone would. But do you really want us to give up everything we do?"

Chelsea sat on her bed. She picked at a loose thread on her blouse. "No . . . I guess not."

"Next time you want to go somewhere special, ask me a few days ahead so we can plan for it. All right?"

Sometimes, she hated the patient way her mother treated her. Sometimes she wished her mother would get mad and yell at her, then hug her. She wanted to sit in her mother's lap and listen to a fairy tale the way she'd done when she was little. She wanted to be a little girl again—when she could see.

Finally, she said, "All right."

She could hear her mother fussing around the room, cleaning up the messy dressing table.

"So, what are you going to do today?" her mother asked.

"I don't know."

"Why don't you ask some of your other friends to come over? There are plenty of things in the refrigerator for lunch."

"Don't worry about me. I can get along just fine."

Her mother gave her a hug. "I know you can, dear. Now, I have to go. I'll try to get back in time to take you shopping."

* * * * *

When everyone had gone, Chelsea sat in her room for a long time. I don't care what Mom said, she thought. I'm not going to sit here and wait for someone to lead me around. I don't need them. She picked up her cane, then threw it on the bed. And I don't need this dumb thing either.

Chelsea got her shoulder bag, put her wallet in it, fumbled in the closet for her jacket, and left the house. She was tempted to take Midnight, but no dogs were allowed in the mall.

Just before she reached the end of the drive, she stopped and mentally pictured the route. Seacrest Drive was a dead-end street, so there was very little traffic. Five blocks. No turns. There was only one busy street to cross, and it had a traffic light. It shouldn't be too hard. So why was she breathing so fast?

She took a tentative step on to the sidewalk, trying to remember all the things she'd learned. Her heart hammered against her chest. For a moment it felt as if her stomach had disappeared and left a huge empty hole in her middle. Maybe I should go back for the cane? No, she thought. The darned thing is long and clumsy and hits everything. I'd be sure to trip someone. If Marty can get around by himself, so can I.

She turned to her right. The wind had come up, but the sun felt warm on the left side of her face. She walked slowly, feeling the hard sidewalk under her feet. Chelsea passed the house next door. She could smell the roses in the yard. She recognized the Miller house because of their large pine tree. The wind sighed through the branches, and she could feel the needles underfoot. Funny, she thought, I never noticed them before.

It seemed like miles until she reached the end of the first street. She listened for the sound of a car. Hearing nothing and seeing no dark outlines, she carefully stepped off the curb. At the other side, she squared her toes to the curb and stepped up. So far, so good.

Two more streets. I'll show them, she

thought. I don't need anybody's help.

The wind tugged at her jacket and blew wisps of hair across her face. Several times she thought she heard footsteps, but she saw no outlines. No one spoke to her. She knew when she passed the old vacant lot on Neptune Drive. The open field gave back no echoes.

She was moving along confidently when something crashed nearby. Startled, she swung around and nearly lost her balance. "Who's there?" she asked. She waited for a moment. When no one answered, she moved forward slowly. Using her bent right arm to protect herself, she felt ahead of her with her left hand. Another gust of wind brought another loud crash. This time she recognized the sound of metal against wood. She let out a gasp of relief. Feeling silly, she realized it was the old FOR SALE sign on the lot.

For a moment she was turned around. Then feeling the sun on her left side again, she headed for the mall.

At the busy intersection, she stood a long time listening to the sounds of the cars. After a few minutes, she could tell when the traffic stopped and resumed. But what if someone made a right turn just as she started across? she thought. She heard someone speak, but she didn't know if they were talking to her.

She wished now that she'd brought the cane. At least maybe the drivers would watch out for her.

Just after she got up enough nerve to step off the curb and take a few steps, a jet plane blotted out the sound of the cars. In a panic she stood frozen, afraid to move, afraid not to go on.

Cars honked. Tires squealed. Someone yelled. She rushed back to the curb and stood there shaking, her heart hammering.

"Are you all right, child?" a woman's voice asked.

"I—I can't cross the street."

"Come on, my dear. The light's green again."

The woman took Chelsea's arm and hurried across. "I get scared, too," she told Chelsea. "The way some people drive these days, it's a wonder more of us aren't killed crossing streets."

Chelsea stumbled against the curb.

"Sakes alive, you're blind. You shouldn't be out alone."

Chelsea didn't know which was worse—to have someone think that she was blind or that she was a stupid baby afraid to cross a street alone. "I'm fine now. I just felt a little dizzy before," she lied. "Thanks a lot."

"You're sure you'll be all right?"

"Yes, I'm just going right here to the mall."

Chelsea moved quickly on before the woman could think of more objections.

Now there were more people on the sidewalk. She bumped into someone.

"Why don't you watch where you're going?" a voice asked.

"Sorry," Chelsea mumbled, not even sure the person was speaking to her.

As she drew closer to the mall, people jostled and pushed. At the entrance she stopped. Was it an automatic door? she wondered. She couldn't hear any sound of a door opening and closing.

"Are you going in, or not?" an impatient voice asked.

She stood aside. Still no sound of a door. It must be open. Holding her arm in front of her, she felt her way forward. Once inside she stood for a moment to get her bearings, trying to visualize the mall. Luckily, Teen Alley was on the street level. The thought of the escalator petrified her.

She remembered she had to turn right and go halfway down the other end of the mall. As she walked along, she realized she could tell some of the places by the odors and sounds. The Bath Boutique smelled of soap. The Record Center blared rock music. The Sweet Shoppe smelled of chocolate. And the flower shop's air conditioning blew wet, flower-scented air through the mall.

Something soft hit against her legs. A child cried. "I'm sorry," Chelsea said, peering down, trying to see the outline.

"Timmy, I told you not to run." A young woman's voice sounded irritated and tired.

"Can you tell me where Teen Alley is?" Chelsea asked.

"Oh, I think it's back the other way. I'm not positive though—Timmy! Get back here!"

As the woman pushed past, Chelsea was jostled by someone. Someone else bumped her, turning her part way around. Now she wasn't even sure if she'd started in the right direction. Maybe it was to the left of the entrance. Her eyes brimmed with tears of frustration.

"Watch it, young lady!" a man's voice said as he pulled her backward. "You nearly hit the potted tree."

The voices became a roar in her ears. The sounds, the blurred movements, the crowd, all closed in on her. In a panic, unable to breathe, she felt as if she were in a nightmare. She wanted to cry out for help, but no sound would come out. With both arms stretched out in front of her, she rushed headlong through the crowd until she touched glass. She felt along it. It was a plate glass window.

"May I help you?"

"I—yes." Chelsea took a deep breath to calm herself. She smelled doughnuts. "Is this—the Doughnut Hole?"

"Sure is. Are you okay?" The voice came from a girl, probably older than Chelsea. "Oh, hey, you're blind, aren't you?"

"No! I—yes," she finally admitted. "Please, do you have a phone I can use? It's an emergency!"

"Sure. Come on in. Give me the number and I'll call for you."

Chelsea gave the girl the number of her father's office. In a moment, the girl put the receiver in Chelsea's hand. Unable to control the tears now, she could only cry, "Oh, Daddy! I need you. Hurry!"

Eight

CHELSEA huddled in the front seat of her father's car. She waited for him to bawl her out for going to the mall alone. Instead, he was silent on the short trip home until they pulled into the drive. She started to open the door.

"Wait, Chelsea," he said quietly.

"But don't you have to get back to the office?"

"No, I told the client I'd see him Monday. You and I need to talk."

"Daddy, I'm sorry. I know I shouldn't have gone out alone."

"That's not what I want to talk about, sweetheart." He took her hands in his. "We haven't really talked since—since all this business with your eyes."

For the first time, Chelsea realized that her father had been trying to pretend that she was just the way she'd always been. "Daddy, why don't you just say it? I'm blind—legally blind. I was really stupid today. I just plain can't do some of the things I used to do." She'd wanted so badly to be independent like everybody else. But she guessed that being independent didn't mean being foolish.

"I haven't wanted to admit it," her dad said slowly. "It hurts too much. But I've been thinking of my own feelings, not yours."

Her father had never talked to her this way before—as if she were an adult. She had come crying to him for help, and he was treating her like she was grown up.

"You know better than anyone what you're capable of doing," he went on. "But if you do get into trouble again, promise you'll call your mom or me. And I promise not to keep after you about being careful. A deal?"

"A deal." She leaned over and kissed his cheek. "Dad, will you help me into the house? I want to get my cane."

* * * * *

When Chelsea was little, everyone had called her Pumpkin, because she'd been born on Halloween. This year, October 31st came on a Friday, so her mother had suggested they have a costume party.

At first she didn't want a party and only

agreed because she could hide behind a mask. Except for Tina, she had avoided being around the other kids she knew. Or they had avoided her.

She called Tina right away. "Guess what? Mom's giving me a costume party. It's my birthday, but no presents. Help me figure out who to ask."

"Well, Kevin asked you to his party. You have to invite him."

"Okay, but he probably won't come."

"I bet he would if you asked Mickey, too."

Chelsea laughed. "And guess who else wants Mickey to be there?"

They made up a list a six guys and four other girls. "I suppose I should invite Marty Talbot from my class," Chelsea said. "I mean, he's really been nice to me."

Chelsea heard the silence at the other end of the line. "You'd hardly know he's blind," she said. "Even I didn't realize he was at first."

"Well, sure, but who can you pair him with? Maybe you should ask one of the girls in your class, too."

"There's nobody the right age. Anyway, it's not like we're couples or anything."

"Sure, you're right. Now, what about costumes?"

Chelsea had already given that some

thought. "I'm going as a clown." Then if she bumped into things or tripped, she could just pretend it was on purpose. "How about you?"

"I won't know until I see what the costume shop has. I sure don't have time to make anything. I'm having a terrible time with English. Miss Bolton makes us read so much stuff."

"Tell me about it," Chelsea said. "You should try listening to talking books or reading in braille."

"Do you know Monday's assignment?"

"Sure, I have it on tape. I just finished listening to it. We have to read pages 112 to 122."

Tina groaned. "Bolton is a tyrant."

Chelsea heard someone behind her.

"Are you going to be on that phone all night?" Billy wanted to know.

"The twerp wants to use the phone, Tina. I'll see you in the morning. We can make more plans for the party."

* * * * *

On Halloween Chelsea's mother fixed an early dinner with all Chelsea's favorite foods. But Chelsea was too nervous to eat. Her birthday presents from the family were a micro-mini tape recorder, a new rock tape, and a winter coat. Even Midnight got into the act. He brought one of his doggie bones to Chelsea and set it by her feet.

By seven o'clock, Chelsea was almost sick. For the hundredth time she asked her mother, "Do you think anybody will come? Does this costume look dumb?"

The whole family had helped to make Chelsea's clown outfit—baggy pants, a jacket with dozens of pockets and patches, and a pancake-shaped red hat. She was wearing clown makeup and huge dark glasses with green frames.

"I hope I don't trip over these silly feet." They'd taken a pair of size 13 mukluks and painted toes on them.

The doorbell rang. "I'll get it," Billy said.

"Don't forget," Chelsea told him, "if it's one of my friends, be sure and clue me in on the costume."

"It's probably another trick-or-treater." In a minute Billy hollered, "Hey, Sis, it's for you—somebody named Marty Talbot."

"Well, invite him in," Chelsea said. She had asked Marty to come early. She knew he'd want to get used to the house before the others arrived.

"That's a neat pirate's costume," Billy said loudly for Chelsea's benefit.

Chelsea headed for the door. "Hi, Marty,

this is my brother, Bill. Come on into the living room, and I'll show you around." She could just barely see Marty's outline silhouetted against the porch light.

She led Marty to the living room where her mother and father were still setting up some of the games. "Mom, you already know Marty. Dad, this is Marty Talbot from my class at the resource room."

"Glad to meet you, sir," Marty said.

"You two should get along great, Dad. Marty's really into math and computers."

They made polite talk for a moment, but Chelsea was anxious to show Marty how to get around the room. She made a face at her mother, hoping she was looking.

"Marty, excuse us," her mother said. "We still have some work to do. I'm so glad you could come tonight."

Chelsea started at one corner of the room so Marty could feel along the wall.

"I feel a sliding door. Do you have a deck?"

"Uh huh. It looks out over the ocean. I wish you could see it at sunset. It's so beautiful."

"Maybe you can describe it to me some—whoops, what's this, a metal stand?"

"I'm sorry. The light in here is really bad tonight. That's a telescope. You can see whales and ships and—" She stopped. "I'm sorry, Marty. I keep forgetting you've never seen a whale or a ship or a sunset."

"Hey, don't stop talking about things. How else am I going to learn about them?"

"You're right." She showed him the rest of the room. "There's a bathroom just off that hall to your left."

"This room must have really high ceilings."

"They're beamed. The whole place is kind of rustic-modern. There's lots of redwood and glass and stone. The floors are tile and slate, so we don't have to worry about tracking in sand."

When they finished the tour Chelsea whispered, "Mom and Dad promised to stay in the family room." Still whispering, she added, "Do you ever get used to not knowing if someone else is in the room?"

"I still get fooled sometimes. But you get used to listening for sounds. Like right now, your brother Billy is sneaking along behind us."

Billy giggled. "I didn't think you knew I was here."

"I have special radar," Marty said in a deep, mysterious voice.

"Aw, you're just kidding—aren't you?"

"If you don't believe me, come over here and try to touch me."

Chelsea listened, trying to figure out what Marty was up to.

"Go ahead," Marty said. "Try to touch my right hand . . . . Gotcha! Try again."

"Hey, how do you always know when to grab my hand?" Billy sounded puzzled. "Are you sure you can't see anything?"

"Nothing at all."

"Boy, that's neat. Can you box?"

"Only a little. But I'm on the wrestling team."

"Yeah? Could you teach me?"

"Sure. Any time."

"Except now," Chelsea said. "The other kids should be here any minute."

* * * * *

After the first few minutes, the party went fairly well. The kids seemed to enjoy the games, dancing, and refreshments. Tina was dressed as a witch. She was in charge of choosing the music from Chelsea's huge collection of records and tapes.

Chelsea had changed the clown shoes for sandals, but she kept herself busy so no one would ask her to dance. She was afraid to try it.

She asked Tina to help her bring out some more cider. In the kitchen, Tina asked, "Why didn't you tell me Marty was so cute? He's gorgeous."

"Tina, I can't see him. Remember?"

"He has curly hair, a cleft in his chin, and the brownest eyes I've ever seen. I just finished dancing with him. All the girls are practically drooling over him. No wonder you wanted to keep him all to yourself."

"I was kind of worried that the kids would either pity him or ignore him."

"He seems just like any other guy—not weird, or anything."

Chelsea bit back a tart reply.

As they came out to the living room, Chelsea felt a hand on her shoulder. "Guess who?"

Her shoulder tensed. "It's Jack," she said, and turned. "Jack Massey."

"That's really great how you can do that," he said.

Chelsea knew he was only trying to be friendly. "It's not so great, Jack. I've been hearing your voice since I was three."

Someone came up from behind and touched her arm.

"Hey, Chelsea, where have you been hiding?"

She recognized Kevin's voice. "I haven't been hiding," she said. "I've just been busy."

"Want to dance?" he asked.

"It's too fast."

"I'll put on a tape you can slow dance to," Tina said.

Kevin led Chelsea into the center of the room.

"It's a great party. Great music. Next time I give a party, how about bringing some of your tapes?"

"Sure, you can borrow them any time." Or come over here and listen, she started to add, but she didn't.

They talked a little about school and Kevin's four-wheeled cycle. When the song ended, he brought her back to the table.

"Thanks, Chelsea. See you later."

"Chelsea? It's Marty. How about a dance?"

She hesitated.

"It's okay," Marty said. "Everybody will get out of our way."

Marty took her into his arms. Tina had put on another slow, dreamy song. Chelsea was surprised at how easily they danced to the music.

"Are you having a good time?" she asked.

"I sure am. It's the first party I've been to in Seaview. I like your friends."

"I'm glad. Are most of your friends blind?" she asked.

"No. Back home, I was the only blind kid."

Marty's arm tightened around her. Chelsea realized that his cheek was against her hair.

"You sure dance well," she said. "You haven't stepped on my toes once."

She was sorry to hear her mother say, "All right, everybody. Who has room for cake and ice cream?"

There were cries of, "Me." "I can always eat cake and ice cream." "Lead me to it."

"Chelsea, why don't you do the honors and blow out the candles," her mother said.

Chelsea crossed to the table.

Her mother unobtrusively moved Chelsea directly in front of the cake. "Be careful," her mother whispered, "so you don't burn yourself."

Chelsea bent over. She felt the warmth of the candles on her face. And then something deep inside her erupted.

"Mom!" she screamed. "I can't see the candlelight! I can't see anything at all!"

Nine

CHELSEA fled from the room. In her bedroom, part of her mind heard the party break up and the kids leaving. Another part of her mind kept going over and over the moment when she realized she couldn't see the light from the fourteen candles. She sank down on the bed. There was no hope . . . no hope that she'd ever see again.

She heard someone come into the room. Then she felt her mother's arms around her and could no longer hold back the sobs.

"Honey, it's all right to cry. Let it out." Her mother told her, rocking her gently back and forth for a long time.

Finally, there were no more tears. In a choked voice, raw from crying, Chelsea whispered, "I'm really blind now. The doctor said this might happen, but I kept hoping . . . ." Her voice broke again. "Mom, I think I need to be alone now."

Her mother helped her undress, put her to bed, and tucked the blanket around her shoulders. Chelsea felt the gentle kiss on her forehead.

"I'll keep my door open tonight," her mother said. "If you need me, call."

Chelsea nodded. She heard the click of the light switch, but the room got no darker.

For a long time she lay awake, thinking about all the things she'd never be able to do, all the things she'd never see. After a while she drifted off to sleep. In her dreams, she was running from an invisible, screaming monster. She awakened drenched in sweat. The scream still echoed in her ears. Was it day or night? She couldn't tell. She groped for the bedside lamp, then remembered.

For her, the lights were out forever.

* * * * *

The next morning at breakfast, the smell of bacon and eggs made Chelsea nauseous. She asked to be excused. "I don't feel very well. I'm going back to bed."

Her mother followed her into the bedroom. "Chelsea, I think it's time we talked."

"Mom, please." Chelsea flopped down on her bed. "No lectures."

Her mother always knew all the answers,

but not this time. Talk wasn't going to bring back her sight.

"No lectures," her mother said. The springs squeaked on the other twin bed. "But I think you ought to know that when anyone suffers a trauma, whether it's blindness, death, or even a divorce, they go through all the same feelings you're dealing with. They don't believe it's happening to them. They get angry and lash out at family and friends. They close people out and feel depressed."

"But Mom, I was getting along pretty well. Now, it's all back again, just like it was when I first went to the doctor."

"I know. And it's perfectly natural. But you worked your way through it before. You can do it again. Look how much you've accomplished."

Chelsea forced a laugh. "Yeah, I can walk to my room without bashing my face into a door."

"Honey, you don't know how proud your dad and I are. I honestly don't think I could have dealt with this anywhere near as well as you have."

"Oh, sure," Chelsea scoffed. "You know how to do everything." Sometimes it was hard to have a mother who was a teacher and counselor and smart and pretty.

"There's something I want you to know. You've really taught me some things these last months. Sometimes when I'm working with a student who is hurting, I get anxious for fear I can't help him."

"Really?"

"Really. Even when you can see, you still fumble around and make mistakes and want to give up. Last year, I almost went back to teaching. And I still have days when I want to give up."

Chelsea was seeing another side to her mother. "Seeing" another side, she thought wryly. I never realized how many words have to do with sight. Maybe I'll have to learn a whole new language.

"Honey, there's something I want you to do for me."

Chelsea sighed. "Please don't make me call all the kids and apologize for breaking up the party."

"No, it's nothing like that. I just want you to take your tape recorder and put down all your feelings. Let it all hang out as your sister used to say."

"I'd feel stupid doing that."

"You used to write in your diary. It's the same thing."

"Okay." But it won't help, she thought.

"Well, that's the end of the consultation."

Chelsea tried to laugh. "So, how much is your fee, Doctor? Fifty bucks?"

"For you, a special rate—one hug."

Chelsea got up from the bed, put her arms around her mother, and squeezed tightly.

Her mother's voice sounded husky. "Paid in full." Then she stood up and spoke briskly. "All your friends called first thing this morning to see how you were doing. Tina will be over after work, and Marty's coming by this afternoon."

"I can't. . . ."

"Honey, don't shut out your friends and family. We all love you."

"I know. And I guess I should feel lucky. Some of the kids in my resource room have lots worse problems. I just wish I could be more like Marty."

"You still have two more phases to go through before you'll be like him—acceptance, then hope."

Chelsea shook her head. "I don't think I can ever accept being blind."

* * * * *

Chelsea finished taping and set the recorder on the stone bench beside her. Her mother was right. It had helped to talk out her feelings. Exhausted now, she leaned back and let the wind from the ocean blow on her face. The day was blustery and cool, but she was bundled up in her new warm jacket with the hood. The air smelled of seaweed, brine, and the pungent odors from the old crab cannery down by the pier.

She heard Billy talking to someone. "She's right over here on the bench. Maybe later you can show me a few wrestling holds? Okay?"

"Sure. I'd be glad to."

Chelsea recognized Marty's voice. She hadn't realized it was already afternoon.

"Here's the bench," Billy said. "Sis, it's Marty."

"I know. Hi, Marty. Want to sit out here, or is it too cold for you?"

"This is great," Marty said. "I like to hear the sound of the surf. It must be a really high tide."

"You should see the ocean during a storm. Sometimes when the waves crash against the cliff, it sends bits of foam half a mile inland."

"Yeah," Billy said, "it looks just like snow." He shuffled his feet. "Well, guess I'd better get out a pad for us to wrestle on. The floor's pretty hard."

"I'll be in later," Marty told him. "Right now, I'd like to talk to Chelsea."

"Oh, sure. Later, man." She heard Billy run off, then he called, "Oh, I almost forgot. Mom said to tell you she's got some hot chili on the stove."

When the two of them were alone, they

didn't talk for a bit. But it wasn't an uncomfortable or embarrassing silence.

Marty was the first to speak. "I'm really sorry, Chelsea. I know how you must feel."

"Yeah, if anyone does, you sure do. Thanks for coming by. I really know how to put a damper on a party, don't I?"

"I'm not sure everybody realized what happened. It must have been awful for you the last few months, not knowing. . . ."

"I guess deep down I knew, but I wouldn't admit it even to myself."

"When I was little, I used to fantasize that a famous doctor would operate on my eyes and I'd be able to see."

"I feel like such a baby. Marty, you never complain or anything."

"Believe me, I've done my share of complaining. I get frustrated and angry just like everybody else. When I'm really tired, I bump into doors that I know are there." He stopped, but she didn't think he was through. In a moment, he went on. "Sometimes when I've had a rough day, Mom will fix fried chicken, and I can't deal with eating it politely." He gave a harsh little laugh. "And butter and jelly are impossible! I used to plop jelly all over the place. Now, I just tell people I don't like butter and jelly."

Chelsea laughed. "And squeeze bottles are

murder. They're awful!"

"It's hard. But you just have to learn to live with it."

"I'll never get used to being around people."

"Start thinking about your family and sighted friends. Think about how you can help them relax around you. If you keep your eyes facing in the direction of a person's voice, it makes that person feel that you're listening."

"What I hate most is not being able to do all the things I love."

"Like what?"

"Swimming in the ocean for one thing. The last time I tried, I got lost. It was awful."

"That's easy. I put a stake on the beach and tie a long nylon cord to it and around my waist. I can swim for hours. Then, I just follow the cord back into shore and I'm right back where I started."

"Okay, I guess that would work. But Tina and I had planned to compete in the swimming meets this year. I'd never be able to stay in the lane or know when to make my turns."

"Why don't you go talk to Coach Knight? I'll bet he can help you. If I can ski, you can swim."

"Ski? How can you do that?"

"With a buddy who acts as my eyes."

"I don't think I could do that," Chelsea said

doubtfully. "That's scary."

"The first time I skied I thought I'd swallow my heart. I could sense all that emptiness around me. And in snow, the echoes are deadened. Believe me, I was scared spitless."

"So, okay, maybe I can learn to ski and swim in competition, but let's see you figure this one out. All my life I've wanted to be a photographer. Have you any idea how impossible that would be now?"

"I have to admit that's a tough one. We'll work on it."

A wonderful feeling of warmth washed over her. He really understood. Oh, she knew that her family and Tina and her other friends were sympathetic and loved her, but they didn't understand how it felt to be blind.

"Hey, Marty, I'm starved. Could you go for some chili?"

"I sure could. That sound you hear is my teeth chattering."

Chelsea laughed and reached for Marty's hand. His cold hand felt strangely warm and firm as he squeezed hers gently. For a moment, they just sat there. She wished she could see his face. It was so hard to know what another person was thinking or feeling.

She picked up her tape recorder. "Come on," she said. "Last one there has to wash the dishes."

Ten

CHELSEA waited for just the right time to approach her parents about swimming. Last year they'd agreed, but now. . . .

She talked fast. "Mom? Dad? Is it okay if I try to get on the swim team? I'll need a suit and warmups and stuff. And I'll have to spend a lot of time at the pool."

"Absolutely not," her father said. "It's too dangerous."

"Daddy, you promised. Remember?"

"Honey," her mother said gently, "don't you think you have enough to learn just coping with blindness?"

"Marty will help me with my homework. Please? Just let me try."

"Does the coach think you can do it?" her father asked.

Chelsea ducked her head. "I haven't asked him yet. I wanted your permission first."

"All right," her father said, but he didn't

sound too happy about it. "But if your grades go down, you're beached."

"Thanks," she said and gave him a quick hug. "I'll work hard, I promise."

On the way to school, Chelsea asked Tina to take her to see the swim coach.

"What for?" Tina asked.

"I've decided to see if I can still try to get on the swim team."

"You're kidding?"

"Nope. Do you have time right after school?"

"Well, sure, but—do you really think you can do it?"

"I can try. I have almost four months before the first meet. If Coach will let me practice every morning and afternoon, I think I can do it."

"It's winter, Chelsea."

"The water's heated. Don't keep thinking up excuses. Will you take me, or not?"

"I'll take you. You sure have guts, Chelsea. I still bang my head sometimes when I make a turn."

Chelsea laughed. "I'll wear a football helmet."

"You'd better wear the whole uniform, pads and all. Otherwise you'll end up black and blue all over. Those lane markers are pretty hard."

* * * * *

At first Coach Knight wasn't exactly enthusiastic about the idea. "Chelsea, I saw you swim last year. I'm always looking for promising eighth-graders. You're good, especially in the backstroke. But I don't know if I have the time to spend with you."

At least he hadn't said it was a dumb idea. "If you can just get me started, I'll work out every morning and afternoon."

"I'm going to be trying to make the team, too," Tina said. "So I'd be here to watch out for her."

"All right," he said, sounding resigned. "Be here tomorrow at six-thirty sharp. I can give you about an hour then and two more after school."

"Thanks, Coach. You won't be sorry."

"I hope not. If your teachers start getting on me because your grades drop, you'll be ineligible."

Fathers and coaches are too much alike, Chelsea thought.

The next morning, Chelsea and Tina were showered and ready at six-thirty sharp. There was a light mist, but the air didn't feel too cold. Chelsea took a deep breath of air. She loved the smell of the water and the feel of the cement on her bare feet.

The coach helped her find the ladder. "Now, the lane you'll use is to your left as you go down."

She felt along the side so she'd know how far it was from one lane to the next. She tried to visualize the pool, the blue and yellow coiled lines that separated the lanes. She remembered the blue and yellow backstroke flags overhead, but they would be no help to her now.

"Here's the center, right by the bubbler. Now practice pushing off," the coach told her. "See if you can stay in the middle of the lane."

The first time, she banged into the left lane line. She tried again, first lining up against the bubbler, then pushing off. This time, she hurt her right hand on the line.

The coach called, "Come on back. Use the raised black tiles in the center of the lane to get your bearings. You should be able to feel them with your feet."

Chelsea touched the tiles with her toes, then swam back to the start.

After nearly an hour of pushing off, he let her try to swim fifteen strokes. "Just use the crawl for now. Listen for my whistle so you don't bump the wall coming back."

She counted fifteen strokes, turned around, and promptly banged her head into the lane line. Tina was right about needing protection.

Feeling totally disoriented now, she tried to find the center of the lane again. This wasn't going to be so easy after all.

Tina swam up to her. "Do you still want to do this?"

"Sure I do."

Just then she heard voices near the starting block. As she swam closer, she heard a boy say, "Hey, is that girl blind? Man, that's crazy."

"Yes, I'm blind," Chelsea said angrily, "but I'm not deaf!"

The coach's whistle cut off her next remark.

"That's all for now, girls." He helped Chelsea out of the pool. "You did much better than I thought you would, Chelsea. But your right leg seems to be stronger, and it makes you veer to the left. This afternoon I want you to practice with the pull buoys and a kickboard." Then he said for Chelsea's ears only, "Don't let the kids bother you. They'll get used to the idea."

I just hope I do, Chelsea thought.

* * * * *

Chelsea dropped the ping-pong paddle on the table. "Billy, I'll never get the hang of this again."

"Just one more game, Sis. You never have

time to do anything with me any more."

Chelsea sighed and picked up the paddle. "One more and that's all. I have to work on my 'oral presentation' as Mrs. Bolton calls a speech."

Chelsea served, then listened for the sound of the ball on Billy's paddle. She managed to hit his return, but the ball went into the net. She served again, and this time she won the point.

As usual, Billy won, but at least she'd made a game out of it. Chelsea was determined to re-learn the game and get as good at it as Marty. He was amazing. She was beginning to think Marty could do anything he made up his mind to do, except maybe be a surgeon!

If it hadn't been for Marty, Chelsea would never have kept up with her classes. He helped her learn braille in record time. And he managed to make the visual aids seem simple to use. Often, he came by the pool and walked home with Chelsea and Tina. He always claimed it was to teach Billy how to wrestle.

Tina didn't buy the excuse. "Marty likes you." She sighed sadly. "I sure wish he had a brother."

Marty had been right about dealing with other people. The better she learned to get around, the more self-confident she felt. A few of the kids still teased her, but most of the ones in her regular classes were helpful and friendly. Some of them called her for help or to get assignments they'd forgotten. They knew Chelsea would have them on her recorder. She liked being able to help someone else.

Chelsea was surprised at how well she was doing in English and history. They had always been her best subjects, but she had thought it would be harder now. It just took more time having to listen to talking books instead of reading. And by helping Chelsea edit her papers for typos and errors, Tina was doing better than ever in English this year. "I might even get a *B* for a change," Tina had said happily.

* * * * *

As they were headed for Mrs. Bolton's room on the day of oral presentations, Tina was going through her notes. Chelsea was going over her speech in her head. She practically knew it backward and forward but was worried she'd forget.

At the door of the English room, Tina said, "Wish me luck."

"Me, too," Chelsea said and moved confidently to her seat.

Mrs. Bolton started at the end of the alphabet, so Tina had to give her speech first.

She made a few little mistakes, but did well.

Chelsea barely listened to the others. She kept going over her own presentation. *Every short story must have conflict and decisions. There are three main conflicts: man against man, man against self, man against nature.* Then she heard her name.

She made her way to the front of the class. She talked for a few minutes about the construction of a short story. Then as an example, she had written a short story called "Murgatroyd the Friendly Mole."

Chelsea took a deep breath and began the story. "Murgatroyd was a star-nosed mole with twenty-two pointed feelers around his snout. Like all moles, he could only see well enough to tell day from night, but he got along just fine. He lived in a large marsh and was a very good swimmer. In fact, he was thinking about going out for the school swim team, The Stars.

"But Murgatroyd was very unhappy because all the other moles were unfriendly. He was never sure if they were just unsociable or if they didn't like him."

Chelsea got so involved with poor Murgatroyd's problems that she forgot everything else. When she finished, there wasn't a sound in the room as she took her seat. But as she passed down the aisle, she sensed her classmates' approval and knew her speech had been a success.

* * * * *

Chelsea was feeling fairly good about herself, when she realized that Christmas was only a few weeks away. Her family always made a big deal out of Christmas. She wished she could go hide in a cave until after the holidays. But Christmas was pretty hard to ignore with carols on every radio station and resounding from supermarkets and stores.

Sharon was home for the holidays, and she and Chelsea were in the kitchen helping their mother with lunch.

"Mom, I don't know how I'm going to be able to give any presents this year," Chelsea said. "Now that I'm not picking ferns, the only money I have is my allowance."

"My gosh," Sharon said, "nobody expects you to give presents." Her tone said, nobody expects a "blind" person to give gifts.

Chelsea had enough money to buy something for her mother, father, and Sharon. She planned to give Billy her camera. But she was stumped for gift ideas for her grandparents, Tina, Marty, and the kids in her resource class.

Her mother came up with a suggestion. "I have a recipe for no-bake cookies that taste like fudge. With a little help from Sharon, you could easily make them."

"Hey, that's a great idea," Chelsea said. "Sharon, can we start right after lunch?"

Her sister moaned. "I'm supposed to meet Eric this afternoon. Can't you get Tina to help you?"

"She's gone to Bay City for two weeks to visit her grandmother."

"I'll clean up the dishes before I go shopping," her mother said. "Sharon, you can certainly take time to read her the recipe, find the ingredients, and get her started."

"I haven't seen Eric for ages," Sharon muttered, then grudgingly agreed.

After lunch, Chelsea got out her tape recorder. "Read the recipe into this," she told her sister.

Before they started, Chelsea washed her hands then reached for the hand towel. The rack was empty. "What did you do with the towel?" she asked. "It's always right here."

"It's right there on the count—I'm sorry. I keep forgetting."

Sharon got out the sugar, cocoa, oatmeal, peanut butter, and the rest of the ingredients. Chelsea set each item on a tray so she could find everything. "Is this instant oatmeal or old-fashioned style?" she asked.

"It says fast-cooking."

"And how about the vanilla? Did you get out the imitation or Mom's real vanilla?"

"For gosh sakes, what difference does it make?"

"Plenty. Mom says it takes twice as much of the imitation kind."

"It's the good stuff," Sharon said with an irritated sigh. "Can we speed this up? I'll be here all day. Here, let me measure the sugar and peanut butter."

"No, I can do it. Mom put daubs of glue on one of the sets of measuring cups."

Chelsea crossed the kitchen to get the milk out of the refrigerator and stumbled over the step stool.

"I'm sorry, Chel. I guess I forgot to put it back where it belongs."

Chelsea didn't say anything. Why couldn't people remember? It was hard enough to get around. She silently put the sugar, cocoa, and milk into a pan and stirred it, but when she went to set the spoon on the tray, it clattered to the floor.

"Now look what you've done!" Sharon cried. "There's chocolate all over the cupboards."

Flustered by Sharon's yelling, Chelsea forgot everything she'd been taught. Instead of protecting her face with her arm and bending her knees, she bent over to find the spoon, and banged her head against the countertop.

Sharon helped her up. "Are you okay?"

"I'm fine. Just don't yell at me. It makes me nervous."

"Maybe you'd better let me make the cookies. It'll be faster."

"No. Then the presents wouldn't be from me. Come on, just get me started on this first batch, and then go."

"Chelsea, look, I'm sorry. I just don't see how you can ever learn to cook and do things like this. Maybe I should practice going around blindfolded so I'll know how it feels to be blind."

A cold anger filled Chelsea. "You'll never know what it's like to be blind!"

Eleven

ON Christmas Eve, Chelsea's father always played Santa Claus and handed out the gifts. Chelsea tried to laugh and join in the fun of opening presents, but all she could think about was the way Christmases used to be. She couldn't see the tree, the lights, all the decorations. She couldn't see the expressions on her parents' faces when they opened the gifts from her. She had chosen cologne for her mother, a billfold for her dad, and an album for Sharon.

Chelsea tried not to be disappointed by her own presents, a braille calendar, a talking clock radio, a braille wristwatch, and a braille Scrabble game. She really appreciated them, but they all had something to do with her blindness. There's more to me than just being blind, she thought wistfully.

When Billy opened his present from Chelsea, she didn't need to see his face to know how happy he was.

"Sis! Your camera? You mean, it's really mine?"

"Yes, and you might as well have the other equipment, too. I can't use them." For the first time, she realized she had finally accepted the fact that she was blind. Like Marty had said, no good fairy was going to wave a wand and tell her she could see again.

"Oh, wow," Billy said for about the tenth time. "It's great, Sis. It's—I guess you'd better open your present from me."

Billy put a large box in her lap. Chelsea grinned. "Are you sure it won't explode or jump out at me?"

"No," Billy answered, his tone was serious. "I just hope you won't be mad."

Chelsea realized that everyone had stopped to watch her open the gift. She tore off the paper and carefully opened the box. She felt something like a large book. It was probably a braille book, she thought.

"Open it," Billy said.

She turned the heavy plastic cover and ran her fingers over the page. There were squares of slick paper. Above each square she recognized the braille dots. *Midnight on the beach.* Another one said *Sunset.*

"Billy? These are pictures. But I don't understand."

"Now, don't get sore, Sis. They're all pictures you took."

"They can't be. I threw everything away."

"Yeah. But you left a strip of negatives hanging out of the trash can, and Midnight pulled it out. Jeremy and I saw him, and we took all the stuff out of the can."

"But you had no right. I didn't want any of it around any more."

"I know, but I thought you might change your mind after it was too late. The photo shop developed the last roll of film you ever shot. There's a great picture of Midnight licking Kevin's face. I picked out some of the best pictures, and Marty wrote the descriptions in braille. I figured that way, you could remember what stuff looked like."

Chelsea's throat was so tight she couldn't say anything for a moment. She held the album close, trying not to cry. "Billy, that's the—the nicest—I love it. Come here so I can hug you."

"Agghhh! It's just an old album. You don't need to get all mushy about it."

But she could hear the pleasure in his voice.

She ran her fingers over a photo of a glade where she and Tina had picked ferns. She could almost smell the violets and dank earth, hear the buzz of insects and the murmur of the breeze through the cedars.

"Well, I guess that's the last of the presents," her father said. "Oh, wait a minute, here's one I missed. Chelsea, it has your name on it." Her father brought it to her and put it in her lap.

"Who's it from?" she asked.

"From Santa Claus."

It was a good-sized box, but it didn't weigh very much. She slipped off the ribbon, lifted the lid, and pushed aside the crinkly tissue paper. Her hand touched something incredibly soft. Angora. A sweater. It was an angora sweater like the one she'd wanted to buy at Teen Alley.

"Daddy, it's my sweater." She held it to her face. "Oh, it feels so good."

"It's rose-colored, just like the camellias on the bush out front," he said. "I went back to the mall that evening and bought it. I hope it still fits." He laughed. "You girls keep changing on me."

"I'm sure we can exchange it if it's not the right size," Chelsea's mother said.

Later, they went into the family room. As they did every Christmas, they gathered around the piano. Chelsea's mother began to play "Silent Night."

This isn't such a bad Christmas after all, Chelsea thought. In fact, all in all it's a pretty darn good Christmas.

* * * * *

The next morning, Marty called Chelsea to ask if he could stop by for just a minute. He had a present for her.

Chelsea put a plate of the cookies she'd made on the table in the entryway. Then she slipped on her jacket and sat on the front steps to wait. Out of the wind, it felt almost warm. It wasn't a very Christmassy day, she thought, wondering what it would be like to live where it snowed. It hadn't snowed in Seaview since 1901.

She heard a car drive up and stop. Marty's footsteps on the cement walk sounded brisk and confident. I'll never be able to move like that, she thought.

"Hi, Marty. Merry Christmas. Come on in a minute."

"I can't. Mom and Dad are out in the car waiting. We're having Christmas dinner with friends of my dad's.

"Thanks for putting the braille on my album. It's a great present."

"I was glad to help. Billy was really excited about it." His voice softened. "This isn't much, but I thought you'd like it." He handed her a box. "It's open."

She lifted out what felt like a large shell. It was cool and smooth.

"It's a conch shell. So even when you're away from the ocean, you can still hear it."

She put the shell to her ear and listened. It really did sound like the roar of the sea. "I love it. But I don't have anything as neat for you. Wait just a second. I'll be right back."

Chelsea set the shell on the entry table and picked up Marty's gift. "I made these cookies myself."

Carefully, she held out the plate. "Got it?"

"Yep. Mmm, smells like peanut butter, marashino cherries, and chocolate. Mind if I take a bite now?" A car horn beeped out front. "Guess I'll have to wait. Thanks, Chelsea."

"Me, too. For the shell."

"Merry Christmas," he said, and was gone.

Chelsea stood there for a long moment until she could no longer hear the sound of Marty's car. She put the shell to her ear.

The faint roar made her think of her special rock by the ocean. Some day, maybe I'll take Marty there.

* * * * *

Later that day, Kevin showed up with a fruitcake that his mom had made. Chelsea gave him a plate of her mother's fudge.

Chelsea hadn't talked to Kevin since her party, and she couldn't think of anything to say.

"Well, how are things going?" he asked. "I saw you at the pool the other day. How in the world do you swim in a straight line?"

"I didn't at first. You should have seen my bruises and cuts."

"I'd like to be on the swim team, but basketball keeps me too busy. Hey, come look at the Honda scooter I got for—" He stopped in midsentence. "I'm sorry, I forgot. . . ." His voice trailed off.

Chelsea remembered something Marty had said to her. "It's okay, Kevin. Take me to it, and describe it."

"Better yet, why don't you go for a ride with me?"

"Oh, I don't know. I don't think I could."

"You don't have to do anything. Just sit behind me and hang on. I'll do all the work."

Kevin helped Chelsea climb on the bike. "Okay," he said, "here we go. There's just one rule—no backseat driving."

At first Chelsea felt a little strange. Riding on the scooter was like floating . . . until they hit a pothole. She grabbed Kevin tight around the waist.

Kevin was talking a mile a minute, bragging about the bike, almost as if Chelsea were just any girl, not a blind one.

Chelsea was surprised at how at ease she felt. Maybe it was because Kevin's back was to her, and she knew he wasn't watching her face.

They rode for a while. Most of the time Chelsea had no idea where they were. But then she smelled popcorn. "What's playing?"

She felt his back stiffen. "How did you know we just passed the theater?"

She copied Marty's line. "I have a special radar," she said in a mysterious voice.

"Yeah? Then tell me before we hit the next pothole."

Chelsea was disappointed when Kevin stopped back at the house. As he was leaving, he asked, "Are you coming to see the basketball game Friday—" He stopped, and she could hear the embarrassment in his voice. "I'm sorry, Chelsea, I keep forgetting you're—uh—you can't see."

"It's okay. I might go. Tina and some of her friends are going to the game and to a party afterward. I might go with them. Anyhow, good luck. And thanks for the ride. It was fun. Oh, wait, I have something for you." She went in to get the photo of Midnight licking Kevin's face. "I thought you'd like this," she said.

She heard him chuckling. "You take great pictures."

As she went into the house she was humming. She could hardly wait to tell Tina. Two boys actually seemed to like her. Two boys in one day!

Twelve

"TINA, I had a great Christmas," Chelsea said. "I thought it was going to be awful, especially with you away, but it was super."

On the way to the basketball game, Chelsea and Tina filled each other in about their holidays. They were curled up in the back of the Webb's florist delivery van. The fragrance of gardenias and tuberoses was almost overpowering.

"Did you get a chance to work out at the pool?" Tina asked.

"Yeah, I did. But without you there, someone was always stealing my kickboard or my towels. Tina, I'm getting kind of scared. The first meet is coming up, and I don't know if I'll be ready."

"Coach had a fit because I had to go to Grandma's for two weeks. If I'd known he was going to be so hard on us, I might not have tried to get on the team."

Chelsea didn't agree that the coach overworked them. He'd given up lots of his free time to help her. She changed the subject. "Who's giving the party tonight?"

"Marsha Thomas. I don't think you know her. She's in my science class."

The van stopped. "Here we are, kids," Tina's brother said. "I'll pick you up at the Thomas's at eleven."

Tina helped Chelsea out, and they went into the gym. Chelsea never took her cane where there were lots of people. The game had already started. The yells of the crowd, the referees' whistles, the screech of rubber-soled shoes on the polished wood floor, all bombarded Chelsea's ears. The sounds echoed and reechoed from the high ceiling. She could barely hear Tina over the cheerleaders. "Stand up! Be proud! Shout it! Out loud! We are the Dolphins!"

"Come on, Chelsea. I see a couple of seats up on the sixth row. Do you think you can climb up there?"

Chelsea tried to visualize the bleachers. The open space between the risers was a scary thought. What if she slipped? She took a deep, steadying breath. "I can make it."

Although she felt disoriented, Chelsea managed the steps all right. But their seats were in the middle of the row. She had to walk in front of a dozen outstretched legs.

"Watch where you're going!"

"Sorry."

"Down in front!"

"Sorry."

"That's my foot you're stomping on!"

"Sorry, sorry. Pardon me."

Finally, they made it, and Chelsea sank down on the hard bench. People around her kept jumping up. Tina screamed in her ear. "Kevin just made a basket."

"What's the score?" Chelsea asked.

"Eighteen to fifteen—our favor."

Chelsea wished she'd brought a radio so she'd have some idea of what was going on. Sometimes the local station broadcasted the games. She tried to pretend she was enjoying the game. She yelled loudly whenever Tina did.

At half time Tina asked her if she wanted to get a hot dog. "My treat," Tina said.

But the thought of trying to navigate the steps was too much. "I'd rather stay here. But how about bringing me back one—with everything on it."

By the time Tina returned, the second half had already started. "Hold out your hand," she said. "It's kind of gooshy, so be careful."

Just as Chelsea grasped the sandwich, the

person on her right jumped up and knocked her arm. The hot dog landed in her lap.

She felt Tina brushing off her jeans. "It's not too bad," Tina said, "but the hot dog's had it. Want me to get you another one?" Tina asked, but with a great lack of enthusiasm.

"No. I just lost my appetite."

Chelsea sat quietly through the rest of the game, trying unsuccessfully to be a part of the excitement and fun. By the sound of the crowd, Chelsea knew Seaview was winning. She was glad for Kevin.

As soon as the game was over, Tina helped Chelsea down from the bleachers. "Wait here," Tina told her. "I have to find Maryanne Decker. We're supposed to ride with her parents."

Before Chelsea had a chance to say anything, Tina was gone. The crowd swarmed around her. People jostled and pushed her, spinning her around. She found herself being pulled along with the crowd. The din of voices seemed even louder than during the game. It was so noisy, she couldn't use her hearing to orient herself.

In a panic now, flailing her arms to keep her balance, she called, "Tina! Tina! Tina!"

"I'm right here," Tina said, out of breath. "But I thought I told you to stay put. Come on, Maryanne's waiting out front."

"I feel like I'm a mess. All I can smell is mustard and relish."

"Don't worry about it. I'll help you clean up at the party."

* * * * *

But they were late getting to the party. Most of the other girls were already there.

Someone came up to Chelsea. "Guess who?"

Chelsea was getting pretty sick of the "guess who" game. "I don't recognize your voice."

"It's Becky Anderson—remember, from ballet class?"

Chelsea hadn't seen Becky in ages. "It's nice to see you again."

"Did you know you have catsup and mustard and a revolting green guck all over your front?"

Chelsea hadn't cared much for Becky before, and she liked her even less now. "Sure. I look good in everything I eat."

Chelsea heard laughter. Then someone whispered, "Poor Chelsea, isn't she great? She's so cheerful."

There was another loud whisper. "What do you mean 'great'?"

"Didn't you know? She's blind."

"I wonder if she knows sign language."

Chelsea gritted her teeth to keep from shouting, I'm blind not deaf.

Tina took Chelsea into the bathroom to clean up. It smelled sickeningly sweet from air freshener. "Here," Tina said, "I'll wash you off." But she didn't wring out the washcloth enough, and Chelsea's shirt and jeans felt wet and cold.

Chelsea would have rather stayed in the bathroom, but Tina pulled her out to the living room and settled her in a big chair. "Just call me if you need anything," Tina told her. "I'm going to talk to Marsha for a sec."

Chelsea sat there with a fixed smile on her face, listening to some of the kids talk about new soap opera stars and TV shows she'd never heard of. Voices whirled about her. She was never sure who was talking or where they were in the room.

"Did you see that black jacket in Teen Alley's window?" one girl asked. "I'll just die if I can't have it."

"Did you see the new algebra teacher? He's so cute."

"Yeah. I hate algebra, but I'm going to take it next year."

"You want cute? How about Kevin Gerrard tonight? Twenty-eight points!"

"Are those basketball points or how he rates

on a scale of ten in the looks department?"

Everybody laughed, and Chelsea felt totally left out. She rubbed the plush fabric of the chair arm until it felt warm. Then she cleared her throat.

"Have you heard "Rock Fever" by the new group Blaze?" Chelsea asked, trying to enter into the conversation.

"Oh, I saw the video," someone said. "It's really wild."

"You should see Chelsea's record and tape collection," Tina said quickly. "I think she knows the words to every song in the world."

But the girls continued to talk about new videos. After a bit, Chelsea tried again to join in.

"Have any of you heard that new radio talk show on KCVU?" she asked. "It's really funny. I mean, you should hear some of the weird people who call in."

Nobody said anything. It was frustrating not to be able to see their faces and their reactions—not to be able to judge the silences. She couldn't tell if anyone was even listening to her. "Like last night," she said, and knew her voice was too loud, "this character called and said he was Adolph Hitler's grandson. . . ." her voice trailed off. Why did I say that? she thought. I never listened to talk shows when I could see. They must think I'm as weird as the guy who called in on the radio program.

Marsha broke the long silence. "Tina, do you think Chelsea would like some popcorn?"

Why don't you ask me what I'd like? Chelsea wanted to scream out.

Tina sat on the arm of Chelsea's chair and whispered, "If you want to leave, I'll try to get hold of my brother."

"No, it's okay." She didn't want to spoil Tina's fun.

But for the rest of the evening, Chelsea sat in stony silence, praying for her new watch to tell her it was eleven o'clock.

* * * * *

On Monday, Marty came by the pool to walk home with Chelsea, as he often did when Tina had other plans. Sometimes they played braille Scrabble, listened to Chelsea's music tapes, or walked on the beach when the weather was nice. Mostly, though, they did their homework together.

"Well, are you ready for the first meet next week?" Marty asked as they headed for her house.

"I'm as ready as I'll ever be, I guess."

"I heard some of the kids talking. They can't believe how well you're doing."

"Oh, I'm doing just great at the pool, but

you should see me at a party."

She told him what happened. "I do okay with one person, but I'm never going to another party. I hate them. It's like sitting in one of those rooms with a window of one-way glass. People can see in at me, but I can't see out."

"It's up to you to make your friends feel comfortable. They're even more embarrassed than you are."

"That's pretty hard to believe."

"It's true. I've been dealing with it all my life. You have to ask, 'Were you speaking to me?' And tell your friends to use your name when they talk to you."

"You never seem to have any trouble with people."

"Early on I decided to be a 'good blind kid.' I tried to help other people feel at ease. Sometimes it means I have to accept help whether I want it or not."

"I hate asking for help. I know Tina gets sick of watching out for me. And so does Billy. Every time I think I'm getting along fine, something happens—like that darn party."

"There are a couple of things I do that help me. I like to shake people's hands when I meet them. I can sometimes tell that they're as nervous or embarrassed as I am. Knowing that makes me feel more at ease. And I try to look in the direction of the person talking. My mom worked hours and hours with me to keep me from rolling my eyes back in my head or letting them just wander. I guess that really puts off sighted people."

"Boy, Marty, I don't know how I'd have gotten along without your help. You're the only one I can talk to. Sometimes I get really burned at sighted people, even my family. When Sharon was home for the holidays, she kept moving things."

"What I hate is sitting through a TV show and figuring out pretty well what's happening, then the whole last scene is resolved without a word." He groaned. "It's frustrating."

"And I really resent it sometimes when my friends are complaining about some little dumb problem."

"And how about when they leave the room and you're still talking and you don't know you're talking to yourself." Marty laughed. "Well, now that we got all that out of our systems, how about a game of Scrabble?"

"You're on. And this time I'm going to beat the socks off you."

Thirteen

CHELSEA did well during the two-week tryout period for the swim team. Her times were in the 38.7 or 38.8 bracket for 50 yards. When she heard that she and Tina had both made the freshman team, she was too excited to even talk straight when she told Marty. "I did it. I tamed the mede—I mean, I made the team." She laughed and hugged him. "I think my tongue just went blind, too."

"That's great, Chelsea. I knew you could do it."

Chelsea's mother bought her a blue and gold lycra team suit and new warmups. She loved the feel of the silky suit. She loved everything, even the grueling practice sessions. She went around feeling as if she were flying. The sea gulls had nothing on her . . . until the first meet.

Everybody came to watch—her family, Marty, and probably half the town was there, if the noise echoing off the pool was any indication. Even Kevin came up and wished her luck.

Tina came in fifth in the butterfly and was so excited she dropped her good-luck teddy bear into the pool.

Chelsea was one of the last to swim the fifty-yard backstroke on the junior varsity team. By then, the noise and excitement had made her nervous. She forgot everything she'd learned. Her start was slow. She banged her head on the turn and hit the lane lines twice, which slowed her even more.

She came in last.

On the ride home, no one said much. Later, Chelsea's father asked her to come into his study. "I'd like to talk to you."

She sat on the edge of the leather settee, afraid of what was coming.

"Chelsea, maybe you'd better give up competition swimming and concentrate on school."

"No!" Then she heard him laugh. "Dad, you said that on purpose, didn't you?"

"I know you're not a quitter."

"I can do better. I just need to practice more."

"What do you say I help you on Sundays? I was a pretty mean backstroker in my day."

Her father had been the one to teach her

the backstroke when she first started swimming. "But, Daddy, this is your busiest time of the year."

"I'm not too busy when it's something this important to you. Tomorrow, we'll spend the day working on your kick. I noticed your right leg seems stronger. I think that's why you keep veering into the left lane lines."

"That's what Coach says. He's had me working on the weights. But when I get excited, I forget."

"Well, I have some ideas. We'll go to the Fitness Center and work on the machines. Together, maybe we can do it."

* * * * *

At each meet Chelsea improved her position. By March, her times were in the 35 second range. And once she finished in second place. Near the end of the season her times were down to 33.6. The team was looking forward to an invitational relay in Port City. They had already earned the eighty-dollar entrance fee with a swimathon and a car wash. The team got together to make posters to take to the meet. BLOW 'EM OUT OF THE WATER. SWIM FOR THE WIN. Chelsea wasn't much help making the posters, but she brought cookies that she'd baked.

One day Chelsea was just climbing out of the water after a long practice session when Coach Knight called to her. "I want to talk to you before you go home, Chelsea."

"Sure. What is it, Coach? I know I didn't make that last turn very well."

"You're doing just fine. In fact, that's what I want to talk to you about. Jeanne, one of our backstrokers on the relay team just went to the hospital with appendicitis. I'd like you to take her place on Saturday."

"But, Coach, she's varsity. I'm JV."

"Your times have been coming steadily down. If I didn't think you could help the team, I'd never ask you. You'll start the relay. I'll get permission to have Tina help you out so the area is clear for the second swimmer."

She just stood there shivering, unable to say a word. Coach laughed. "Chelsea, you're hyperventilating. Go get dressed now."

Chelsea managed a thank-you. "I won't let you down, Coach."

* * * * *

On the day of the invitational, Chelsea's father drove her to the school bus. She hadn't told her family she was going to swim the varsity relay. She was afraid of disappointing them if she let the team down.

As she started to climb out of the car, her dad handed her something soft. "I noticed all the other girls have a good-luck animal. I found one that looks exactly like a miniature Midnight."

Chelsea held the small stuffed animal to her face. "Thank you, Daddy . . . for everything."

The school bus horn sounded, and Chelsea, clutching her good-luck dog and her duffle bag, climbed out of the car. She let her father take her to the bus. "Good luck, honey."

During the twelve-mile ride to Port City, Chelsea sat silent, only half listening to the laughter and joking of the rest of the kids. She ran her fingers over the soft furry animal. She was going to need more than good luck today. She and the three others had worked hard all week, but she knew they were worried about her. *Please, God, don't let me ruin it for the team.*

When they scrambled off the bus and found the pool, the coach checked to see if everyone had plenty of towels. Tina showed Chelsea around, warning her of hazards, such as the timer cords and benches and roped off areas. As soon as Chelsea felt comfortable, Tina went to help put up the signs. Chelsea began her stretching exercises, then swam for a while, getting used to the pool and the wall, and preparing herself mentally. Then she dried off and bundled up in her warm-up jacket to wait for the meet to begin at nine.

Just before the first event, Coach Knight gathered everybody together at one corner of the pool for their team cheer. One of the boys took his usual spot on the end of the diving board to lead the cheer. The back of Chelsea's neck tingled with excitement. From different parts of the pool she could hear the other teams giving their yells.

There were eight teams competing. The junior varsity girls were first. The rest of the kids were milling about, yelling for the swimmers. Chelsea huddled on a bench listening to the screaming and shouting, wishing she could see what was going on. Tina kept running over to tell her how they were doing.

By ten-thirty, Chelsea was too nervous to sit still. But she was afraid to go to the snack bar or to the bathroom for fear she'd get lost. Anyway, with all the yelling, starting guns, and whistle blowing, she might not hear them call her event.

At eleven-thirty, the coach rounded up the four backstrokers and gave them a pep talk. He finished with, "Just do your best. And have some fun out there."

Chelsea gave her good-luck animal to one of her timers. "Watch this for me, will you?"

As she pulled on the tight cap and the goggles, her stomach was doing the butterfly stroke. Her throat felt as if she'd swallowed an entire package of cotton balls.

And then it was time.

The starter's whistle shrilled. "Varsity girls backstrokers, go to the block."

The coach took Chelsea to the starting block in lane six.

"Backstrokers, into the water," the starter called.

Chelsea, with her heart pounding wildly, climbed down the ladder.

"Timers—to your watches. Take your mark."

Chelsea positioned herself in the center of the lane, found the backstroke starting bar, and pulled her knees up into position.

The gun went off.

Chelsea got a fast kick-off. "Go for it, Chelsea!" she heard Tina shout.

As she concentrated, counting the strokes to the turn, the yelling faded. She was in a silent, dark world of her own. Nothing else in the world was as important as these few seconds. Nearing the wall, she heard someone screaming, "Come on, Chelsea! Come on!"

It felt like a good turn. But how far was she behind? If only she could tell where everyone was. I have to go faster, she thought. *Faster.*

Don't let the team down. *Faster.* Give everything you've got. *Faster. Faster.* Almost there.

"Come on, Chelsea! Chelsea! Chelsea! Chelsea!"

Finally, she reached the finish. Gasping for breath, she scrambled out. "How'd I do?"

"Great," Tina said. "You made the others look like they were treading water." Tina put a towel around Chelsea's shoulders and gave her a quick hug. She handed Chelsea her warm-ups. "I'll be right back," she said. "I want to see the rest of the relay."

It was awful standing there, unable to see how her team was doing. Then there was a scream beside her. Someone grabbed her and swung her around in a little hopping dance. "Chelsea, we did it! We did it!"

Someone else hugged her. "You got us off to a super start. We did it!"

The coach gave them their times. "We placed first, girls."

She had actually helped the team win. *First place . . . first place.* I'll never, never forget this day, she thought.

As Chelsea got her plush dog from the timer, she heard her mother's voice. "Honey, we're so proud of you."

"Mom! Why didn't you let me know you were here?"

"We were afraid we'd make you nervous."

"You remembered everything you've been taught," her father said.

"It was my good-luck dog," Chelsea told him.

"Sis, I got a picture of you at the finish. I'm going to get it framed."

A hand took hers. It was Marty.

"Chelsea, I couldn't see how you were doing, but I could sure tell by your folks' yelling. Your mom nearly broke my eardrums."

Happy tears filled Chelsea's eyes. "Our team did it, but I couldn't have done my part without my 'home team.' Thanks, Mom, Dad, Billy, Marty."

"What about me? Am I just so much cottage cheese?"

"Sharon! I didn't know you were home from college."

"I got here late, but I saw you swim." Sharon hugged her. "Just don't get too much of a swelled head. I still get my half of the closet!"

Chelsea thought she had never been so happy . . . not even when she could see.

* * * * *

On a warm Saturday just before school was out for summer vacation, Chelsea, Marty, and

Midnight were walking on the beach. The tide was just going out, so Chelsea decided it was time to share her special place with someone who was very special, too. "Come on," she said. "I'm taking you somewhere, but you have to promise you won't tell anybody about it."

"I promise. What is it, a pirate's cave?"

"Almost. Take my hand and follow me closely."

Visualizing every step, she led him through the cave. "Now, careful here. These rocks are really slippery."

When they finally reached her special rock, they sat quietly for a bit, just breathing in the smells of the sea and listening to all the sounds. "I love it here," she said. "I used to spend hours taking pictures." She sighed. "I haven't been here since. . . ."

Marty groped for her hand. "Let me see your face, Chelsea."

"That's a crazy thing to say, you know."

"It's not crazy. I want to see you—the only way I can see you."

He touched her face, gently running his fingers over her cheeks, her eyes, her hair. "The way your hair grows to a point on your forehead, your face is just like a heart. You're beautiful, Chelsea," he said simply.

She didn't know what to say. No boy had ever told her that she was beautiful. "The only thing about me I ever liked much were my eyes, and now . . . I don't know what they look like."

"People are always talking about the color of eyes. What color are yours?"

"Gray."

"Gray? What is gray?"

"Well, this rock is dark gray. A pussy willow is silver gray. There are lots of shades of gray."

"What are shades, Chelsea?"

"You know how there are lots of different flower smells or flavors of ice cream? Each color has a shade."

She wished she could see his face to tell if he was putting her on. If he was serious, how in the world could she describe color to someone who had never seen the brilliant, shiny green of a holly leaf, the pure whiteness of new snow, or the bright red of a fire engine?

"Okay," she said after some thought, "my eyes are gray like the early morning before the sun comes up, or a day when there's no sun. But they're clear like fresh creek water—oh, Marty, it's impossible to describe colors."

"Try."

"Well . . . green is like—like the woods, kind of cool and fresh. Like pine trees or Christmas trees."

"Like pine air freshener?" he asked.

She laughed. "Not exactly. Let's see, red and orange are like the flames in a fireplace. And pink is like the soft petals of a rose or like a blush—" She stopped, feeling her own face flush. "I can't describe colors."

"Then tell me what you used to see when you sat here taking pictures."

Out of habit, Chelsea closed her eyes. "Well, I liked to get up early. Midnight and I used to sneak out of the house before dawn. There's an early morning mist that feels soft on my face. You know, like a—a—"

"Like a gentle kiss," Marty said softly.

Chelsea felt her face turn pink again, and she hurriedly went on. "The smell of the cedars along the cliffs overlooking us is strong in the early morning. I love the trees that are all bent away from the ocean because of the wind. You should see the banks. They're covered with Indian paint brush, pale pink azaleas, Johnny-jump-ups, and purple flags."

"Purple flags? Not red, white, and blue?"

"Flags are a small wildflower—oh, you're teasing me again."

She could hear the smile in his voice. "I'm sorry. I know what they are, I just don't know what they look like. Go on."

Chelsea closed her eyes again. "Whenever the tide has been high during the night, the beach is strewn with smelly seaweed. Insects swarm all over it. When the sun comes up over the hills to the east, everything turns a butterscotch pink. Oh, Marty, it's so beautiful." Impulsively, she reached out.

He took her hand and held it.

"The cave we came through is always cool and dark," Chelsea continued. "A couple of times I've almost been caught by waves at high tide. Along the floor of the cave sea anenomes attach themselves to rocks. They look like flowers. Sometimes I poke at them to see them open and close, like the mouths of fish. Then on this side of the cave, there are tide pools. When the tide goes out it leaves pools filled with skittery bugs and hermit crabs. I even found a poor four-legged starfish once."

They were quiet for a moment. "What's that gurgling sound?" Marty asked. "It sounds a long way off."

"It is. Instead of a sandy beach, the cove is all rocks. The sound is the waves going in and out over the rocks. I've found all sorts of stuff at low tide. Once I saw a child's sneaker among the rocks. There was only one. It was all faded and ragged with no laces. I couldn't help wondering if the little shoe came from around here. Or maybe it came from across the ocean. . . ." Her voice trailed off into silence. Midnight nuzzled against her leg.

"Chelsea," Marty said softly, "maybe you can't take pictures any more, but you could write. You could make word pictures."

"Oh, I don't know about that. It's so hard to put things into words, Marty." She turned toward him. "There's one thing I do know, though. You've made me see in ways I never did before. I mean, really see."

Marty drew his hand away. She heard him sigh. "Chelsea, I guess I can't put off telling you any longer. I—I have to leave Seaview tomorrow."

"A vacation?"

"For good. Now that I've learned how to use all the aids in the resource room, my family can't stay here any longer."

Chelsea felt numb. He couldn't leave. She needed him. Who could she talk to who really understood? "Marty, I don't know how I'll ever get along without you."

"I hate to go. I'm really going to miss you." Then he added quickly, "But we can send cassette tapes back and forth."

It won't be the same, she thought sadly.

He reached out and took her face in his hands. She felt his warm sweet breath as he bent close. Gently, he kissed her, then drew back.

"We'd better go now," he said. "My folks are picking me up at four." His voice was husky. "Thank you for bringing me here."

Silently, with Midnight at her side, Chelsea walked with Marty back through the cave. She shivered a little in the cool dampness, and Marty put his arm around her shoulders.

As they came out the other side of the cave, a sea gull screeched. Chelsea wanted to cry out, too. *Marty is leaving. Marty is leaving.*

The closer they got to home, the slower she walked. She wished time would stop. She wished they could stay here on the beach forever. I'll never forget this day, she thought.

At the top of the stairs Marty stopped and took her hands again.

Chelsea's throat was tight as she whispered, "What time do you leave?"

"Before dawn."

A car horn sounded. "I guess—I guess this is good-bye," he said.

Chelsea swallowed the huge lump in her throat. She tried to keep her voice steady. "I'll be seeing you, Marty."

And now it didn't sound crazy. It didn't sound crazy at all.

If you would like more information about how to prevent blindness, please contact:

The National Society to Prevent Blindness
79 Madison Avenue
New York, N.Y. 10016

Telephone: 1-800-221-3004
In New York: 1-212-684-3505

If you would like more information about resources for the blind or visually handicapped, please contact:

The American Foundation for the Blind
15 West 16th Street
New York, N.Y. 10011

Hotline: 1-800-AFBLIND
In New York: 1-212-620-2147

About the Author

ALIDA YOUNG and her husband live in the high desert of Southern California. She gets many of her ideas by talking with people. She's tried to learn to listen—not just to what people say, but to how they say it. When she's doing a book that requires research, she talks to experts. "Everyone is so helpful," she says. "They go out of their way to help."

Mrs. Young has worked in a soda fountain, a custom picture-framing department, a home for the elderly, and a complaint department for a large store. She has also done work in little theater. Now, when she's writing a story, she puts herself into the shoes of a character just the way an actor would do. She tries to feel all the pain and hurt and all the joy and fun that the characters go through.

Other books by Alida Young include *Why Am I Too Young?* and *What's Wrong With Daddy?*